Steward-Exclamation!

Discovering The Spiritual War

Fifth Segment of the Steward Series

STEWARD-EXCLAMATION!
DISCOVERING THE SPIRITUAL WAR

CHARLES A DE ANDRADE

www.charlesadeandrade.com

Steward Exclamation!: Discovering The Spiritual War

Library of Congress Control Number: 2020914027

About the Author:Raised Roman Catholic with six siblings, Charles married his college sweet heart Gloria in 1973 when both were 20. After college his plans to go overseas to Zambia Africa to teach would be set aside as providence kept him in the US where he became an electrician. Charlie Klein, the electrician who taught him the trade, introduced him to the Biblical Christ. Today, Charles is the proud father of three daughters, the grandfather of eight wonderful grandchildren and one step-son, and he and his wife Gloria live in Summerfield Florida.

Charles currently serves as a board member for Northampton Press/Don Kistler Ministries, publishing Puritan works. He is the founder of Scribblers, a Christian writer's group. He also serves as the President for Bee Natural Products, a company committed to supporting bee keepers and the promotion of their products.

For more information on Charles or his works please see:
www.charlesadeandrade.com
www.charlesadeandrade.com
www.scribblersweb.com.

e-mail him at charlesadeandrade@earthlink.net

This novel is a work of fiction. Names, descriptions, entities, and incidents included in the story are products of the author's imagination. Any resemblance to actual persons, events,and entities is entirely coincidental.

Cover art by Dennis Assayag.

The opinions expressed by the author are not necessarily those of Scribblers Press.

Scripture quotations taken from the New American Standard Bible, Copyright @ 1960,1962,1963,1968, 1971,1972, 1973, 1975, 1977, 1995 by The Lockman Foundation. Used By Permission.

Published By Scribblers Press
Inc. 9741 SE 174th Place Road
Summerfield, FL 34491

ISBN: 978-1-950308-27-9
(Paperback)

Printed by Trinity Press, Inc.
3190 Reps Miller Road Suite 360
Norcross, GA 30071

ISBN: 978-1-950308-01-9 (E-Book)

ACKNOWLEDGEMENTS

It has been many years since the concept of the Steward Series took hold of my mind and heart. As I bring this first series to a close and begin to consider another set of ideas and the new adventure of bringing those into the written world, I am reminded of all the many friends and family that have made this adventure possible.

Without the support of my wife, Gloria, none of this would have happened. She was the first to read my scribblings, and comment on the merits and deficiencies of the stories. Next to my hours, she has spent more time than anyone else reviewing what I was working on. She also has patently accepted the loss of all the time I spent in front of the computer, writing. Thank you my wonderful wife, for your patience, and consistently wise counsel, and the hours you have spent supporting my efforts.

Then there are those family members and friends, who helped me cover the initial cost of getting the first book published. The hoped-for financial return has yet to materialize, but the spiritual return and the experience of seeing that first book in print still fills me with awe. The final four books tumbled forth, out of that amazement.

Thank you to Arol Wolford, Forrest Litvin, James de Andrade, Jan Ulshoefer, Jeanne Litvin, and Jennifer Teter who invested in me and that first book not knowing the outcome.

Not all rewards are necessarily financial in nature, although the hope remains that the financial one will yet occur!

Also, my 92-year-old mother, Pearl de Andrade, has been a faithful part of the editing crew. It is my hope that she will remain for many more years, counseling me on mistakes and improvements to be made to my scribblings. But above all, it has been her faith in Jesus that has been an inspiring experience. Finding family members on that narrow road that takes us to Jesus is one of the most wonderful experiences you can have.

Finally, to me the most amazing part is that our creator put these desires to write in me and provided the opportunity to do so. The apostle John wrote that if everything that Jesus did was written, there would not be enough books in the world to cover it all. (John 21:25). Many probably would call that hyperbole, but my experience would say otherwise, for Jesus is still at work. Each Christian is a part of that story. To me, the greatest promise is summed up in Jesus's statement "…no one will snatch them out of my hand, My father, who has given them to me." (John 10:28- 29) This is saying in my words, "All the Father has given me, I lose not one." How blessed is it, to realize you are one of those ones! Each of us, are a part of that story, and our stories are still being written. The Spirit is still drawing the people the Father has given to Christ. It is my prayer that my stories might also be a part of that grander tapestry that the creator is weaving.

My shout, my exclamation is a thank you to all who have aided me in this first series and me breaking into the doxology that I so love, "Praise God from whom all blessing's flow, praise him all creatures here below, praise him above yea heavenly hosts, Praise Father, Son and Holy Ghost."

Charles A de Andrade, November 2018

DEDICATION

To the faithful men, who proclaimed Christ to me throughout my life. To Charlie Klein, who taught me the electrical trade and displayed the reality of the gospel in his life and in his friendship towards me. He invited me to his church where the gospel was made real. To Mark Pett, at Liberty Reformed Presbyterian Church in Ownings Mill, Maryland, who faithfully proclaimed that word to one whose heart needed changing and accepted with grace the providence that claimed his life so early in his ministry. Both men stand now with Christ. But their impact on my life can not be overstated. God uses sinners turned godly men, to point other sinners to the truth. I am one of them.

To the many other pastors who I have sat under over the years of my life who have impacted me and my thoughts and life. To Dan Broadwater from Grace Reformed Presbyterian Church in Relay, Maryland, John Atkins, Steven Jackson and Rick Holmes from East Cobb Presbyterian Church in Cobb County, GA, Jason Shelton from Providence Presbyterian Church in Salisbury, MD, Bernie van Eyk and Michael Malone of Christ The King Presbyterian Church in Vero Beach Florida, Dennis Rupert of Morningstar Presbyterian Church in Vero Beach Florida, Scott Willet of Redeemer Orthodox Presbyterian Church in Atlanta, GA, Ron Clegg of Parkview Presbyterian and finally Jeff Hosmer and Michael Smith of Northside Presbyterian Church in Summerfield Florida. Some of these men have already departed to stand before the Lord. It is my hope to find them all, waiting expectantly for that Exclamation, that shout when the Lord will return to this earth and bring to completion his plan.

There were others who also participated in my journey who I have not mentioned, with so many explaining God's word to me at various times. Each of these men touched me through the foolishness of preaching and their friendship in walking with me through my life's struggles and dealing faithfully with my sins.

There is a reason why the Lord calls men like these to the life of a preacher. They have been sent to the fields where some sow the good seed into soil prepared to receive that planting, others water the fields that have been sown, and still others are sent to reap the fields that are white…ripe for the harvest.

Exclamation is the story of the ending of the race for one of these pastors whose character is a blend of so many of these men. Like the character in the story whose faithful labor comes to an end, you each will get to experience the Lord coming with the towel and the basin and wiping off the dust of your labor and hearing those words we all long for, "well done my faithful servant, come into the feast prepared for you." Thank you for your labor and for the impact of your work in my life. These stories have been made so much better because of your testimony and faithful exposition of his word.

For our struggle is not against flesh and blood, but against the rulers,against the powers, against the world forces of this darkness, against the spiritual forces of wickedness in the heavenly places.

—Ephesians 6:12 (NAS)

CONTENTS

PROLOGUE

It was the tree. Despite the plentiful display of foliage that draped the surrounding trees with the glorious covering of spring, this tree stood winter time bare. He had noticed that the tree seemed to be dying. He passed the stand of maples almost every day as he drove into town from his home, and this tree stood out from the others on the hill. He was drawn to that tree, examining it from a distance, even as he passed by continuing onwards to work.

Today he had stopped. Now he was certain. The tree was in fact dead.

Sheriff Ken Farr stared upwards at the tree. The slightly swinging figure of the man still embedded in his mind. It was three years since the body was discovered, found by two boys who chose that day to skip school.

They were trying out the new car only recently given to one of them as a reward, for his good grades at the very school they were abandoning for the day.

The man had been tortured. The coroner had described in gruesome detail the evidence of that fact. Much of what was done to the man would never be released to the public. Only a few knew the full scope of the man's suffering. He was alive through the entire experience, according to the coroner. The facts were confirmed by the tape, left at the scene which included an edited recording of portions of his suffering. That tape removed any doubt about just how gruesome the torture had been.

Somehow, it did not seem right that anyone, even this man, should experience such suffering prior to exiting this life. His death was finally accomplished; the burning brand plunged through one of the man's eyes, and deep into his brain. The brand was not removed, but left there, ample evidence of the nature of the final ending act. The agony that final event caused, recorded in all of its clarity, still turned the sheriff's inners, even thinking about it.

The death of Hastings Moment came as a shock to the young sheriff.

Less than a year into his first term as the new sheriff of Hitchenburgh nothing had prepared him for the gruesomeness of this murder.

Ken believed that this one experience proved to him, that there really was a force known as evil. The son of a pastor, he was raised believing in both God and the devil. He had experienced plenty to give credence to the existence of both, but only a very few events came close to proving the existence of one or the other. This killing convinced him that the devil was in fact real. He knew that men, and even women, were capable of incredible levels of brutality, but this murder spoke of something even more. Ken was convinced the murder was done by a person, but what drove that person to do all that was done to this man was something alien to even the most perverse human Ken had ever met.

Hastings was one of the investors that backed Buddy House, the local boy turned entrepreneur, who had started a string of adult entertainment enterprises that now stretched like a noose around several states. The Parlor brought wealth to the sleepy farm town that Ken now was the sheriff of. Buddy's death preceded Hastings by five years. It was Buddy's Parlor that brought the world to Hitchenburgh's doorstep.

The town had been a sleepy farm town, with a main street less than a mile long, anchored by the First Presbyterian Church right at the point where the only two other roads in the town intersected main street. Buddy had built a small airport at the end of Main Street, on a piece of land where he had added Airport Drive, to Main Street, extending the street by another half mile. Because the road jutted off to the right at the end of Main Street, the town fathers had objected to the new addition being called Main Street. That suited Buddy just fine, as he enjoyed the fact that Airport Drive would forever be remembered as one of his contributions to the town.

For years the town had been unknown except to the farmers who found their supplies at the feed and grain shop that doubled as the town's hardware store, got their hair cut at Jerry McCombs Barber Shop that also doubled as the beauty shop where his wife Nanny performed similar functions for the farmer's wives, dropped their kids off at the combination elementary and high school building just up one of the streets intersecting with Main Street, or found a reason to stop for a while to sit in one of the many rockers that lined the walkway running on either side of the street. It was not unusual to see any number of the rockers being used, the farmers and towns folks passing a few slow moments reminiscing about the past or sharing the latest gossip.

Buddy's first Parlor pierced the anonymity of the sleepy town. Suddenly visitors were arriving drawn to the promise of the best evening entertainment at the "Most Friendly Spot" in all of Michigan. It was as if the towns' former seclusion continued, allowing businessmen from both Kalamazoo and Grand Rapids to escape to a place where their participation in the Parlor's entertainment would remain unknown. Money poured into the town, filing the meager coffers of the town's treasury to overflowing. The new-found wealth, increased the need of the sheriff's office, giving Ken his first job as a deputy.

Even after both Grand Rapids and Kalamazoo sprouted their own Parlors, evidence of Buddy's growing wealth and influence, many businessmen still preferred the trip to Hitchenburgh. Many a farmer's daughter had worked at the Parlor, seeking an escape from the farm life that so many now found unfulfilling. It was true, that the farmer's daughters were different than anything the larger cities might offer. There was something alluring in the exposure of formerly pure and protected innocence.

Overnight, many farmers had stopped coming into town, and the once busy rocking chairs, now more often rocked because of the wind blowing. Soon smaller stores were replaced by antique shops, as it became obvious, that a different type of economy had come to the town.

The destruction of the Parlor only a few short days before Buddy was killed brought more attention and sorrow to the town, than anyone in the town had ever experienced. All told, more than forty people were confirmed as missing from that event, nine of them from Hitchenburgh. Ken thought often about the missing friends and citizens, the impact of the Parlor on the town, and the suffering so many families had endured and continued to endure from the Parlor's legacy. Even now, more than five years later, events continued to unfold, some good but many more still pointing to the scaring the Parlor had brought to the town.

Ken's father was at the center of another storm that was brewing, as they all waited the decision from the highest court in the state, about another event directly traced to Buddy's Parlor.

Ken thought again about the psychological profile the experts had given him about the killer. This killing was personal. The victim and the killer knew one another. In fact, one expert had speculated that portions of the torture had likely been played out on the killer by the now deceased victim. There appeared to be some perverse need that was fulfilled in the killer by the torture.

Much of the torture would have been missed by anyone but a coroner. But on the slab, each different aspect of the final hours of the man's life were displayed in all its hideousness. The killer was strong. Wrestling the one-hundred-and-fifty-pound victim from the site of the execution was not an easy task.

Execution.

That was what this killing was. Ken was convinced of that fact by the single other piece of evidence still withheld from the public. The small slip of paper with the man's name written on it, and on the back a well-known bible verse typed neatly. "An eye for an eye" discovered at the execution site later by Ken, a matching brand, a twin of the one removed from Hastings' brain, resting on top of the paper. It had been meant to be discovered. The rest of what was inscribed made no sense to anyone, but "not even in the top ten, what a disappointment" fueled many experts profiles related to the killer.

Ken turned hearing the approaching vehicle. The green truck sporting the logos of the "Tree Doctor" slid up beside his sheriff's car. The sturdy but slender man emerged from the truck and trundled up over the slight hill to where Ken stood.

"Thanks, Henry, for coming," Ken said, reaching at the same time for the man's hand to shake it.

"Not a problem, Ken," Henry replied.

Henry Drake and Ken Farr had known each other their entire lives. Henry had picked up where his father had left off, and now ran the second-generation business that primarily removed trees that needed to be cleared from the new residential lots being carved out of the farm land surrounding the town.   Unlike Henry, Ken had not followed in his father's footsteps. Instead the son of the preacher had become first one of the town's deputies, and then replaced the retiring sheriff three years ago, shortly after the events that had put Hitchenburgh on the nightly news were forgotten, until the murder occurred. But after only a few weeks, that murder was forgotten by the world at large as well, and Hitchenburgh returned to its former anonymity.

"Isn't this the tree?" Henry asked, staring upwards at the now naked maple tree.

"Yes," replied Ken.

"I need you to see, if you can figure out why the tree has died," Ken said.

Henry only stared upwards at the tree. Ken knew he was reliving the same event. It had been Henry who Ken had called to help him get the body down. It was Henry who had found the evidence that someone else had climbed the tree in the recent past. The evidence of the cleats left defining marks on the bark. Unlike Henry's own rubber coated cleats that protected the tree from damage, the cleats the murderer wore were traced back to the type of cleats used by telephone pole workers that left stabbing indentations in the tree. That had started a futile search through all the telephone and electrical firms, looking for any cleat that would have matched the marks left by the murder. Unfortunately, the sheer number of cleats found hid any possibility of discovering a single set that would have made the marks. No one at any of the firms knew of any missing cleats. This piece of evidence quickly shed any potential for unmasking the killer.

"Pretty odd to see a maple like this one die. Most maples will last for upwards of a couple of hundred years, but this one isn't even a quarter of that age, and all of its other siblings are still doing fine," said Henry as he motioned around at the other trees fully decked out in the vivid green foliage of the young spring.

"That's why I wanted you to take a look at it. I want to know if there is something here that we have missed so far, perhaps some other piece of evidence that might shed some light on what happened here," Ken said.

Henry nodded again and then began walking towards the tree. Ken watched from the distance, as Henry circled the tree looking up and down at the tree, as if gauging what had happened. Henry motioned to his truck.

"Would you go grab my climbing belt from the truck Ken, I want to take a look see further up," Henry said.

Ken headed for the truck and found the belt. When he returned, Henry slipped on the belt, and began the quick climb up the tree. When he reached the branches he unhooked his belt, leaving it for his return trip to the ground. It was easy to see why Henry was perfect for this job. A heavier man would have easily broken some of the branches, but Henry seemed to be able to scurry among the branches without causing anything more than a slight swaying. All the time Ken saw that Henry's hands, while covered by sturdy gloves, were still feeling the branches and measuring the branch's strength and searching for any evidence of what had caused the trees death.

After about ten minutes of dancing from branch to branch, Henry started his way back down. Suddenly, he stopped, only about six feet from ground level and stared. Ken watched as Henry removed a knife from his coat pocket and then began to appear to dig out something from the trunk of the tree.

'What did you find?" Ken called up.

"Just a minute," Henry replied.

Henry returned to the ground, carrying the object he had dug from trunk of the tree in his hand.

Ken looked at it. It was a flat headed nail, only about an inch long.

"A nail,?" Ken said, disappointment clearly echoing in his tone.

Henry nodded, and then returned to the tree and began looking around the base of the tree, anywhere from two feet to six feet from the ground.

"Ken, come here," Henry called. Ken slid up beside Henry again, looking at where Henry was pointing. Almost hidden against the trunk was the barely visible head of another nail. Henry pointed again, and slowly together they made the circle around the tree, every two or three inches seeing another head of a nail, already hidden almost completely into the trunk of the dead tree. The greenish head of the nail blended almost perfectly with the bark of the tree. All told, they counted twelve nails.

"Twelve nails?", Ken asked.

"No, Thirteen if you count this one," Ken again holding up the nail he had found just above their heads. Henry returned to his truck and then came back, a small piece of sandpaper in his hand, and started rubbing the nail he had removed. Slowly the tarnish disappeared, and the golden brown hue of the metal was exposed.

Henry held up the nail, for Ken to see.

"A copper nail?" Ken asked. Henry nodded.

"We call these 'tree killers', to the trees the copper is as toxic as arsenic is to us," Henry said.

"Someone wanted this tree dead", Henry said.

"How long have the nails been here?" Ken asked.

Henry shook his head.

"Hard to know, but it would take only one or two seasons for the copper to do in the tree. It was definitely something done after the murder, I think," Henry said, the last two words qualifying the answer as not definitive.

"Why the nail further up the tree, were there others up there?" Ken asked.

"Nope, but as to why further up", Henry opened his hand again, and the small weathered piece of paper fluttered between his fingers.

"Probably should have left it there, for us to take our time removing, but I thought you would probably really want to see this," Henry said.

"And, that thirteenth nail.... it's only been up there for a few months; see the metal, the tarnish it's too thin to have been in the tree for long.

Someone's come back and left a message," Henry said.

Ken kicked himself mentally, as Henry had been right, it would have been better to leave what he had found until they could have potentially left the clue more intact, but Henry's curiosity had won out.

"I was careful, I didn't touch the paper with my fingers, only with the gloved part of my hand," as he handed the piece of paper to Ken.

Ken reached into his pocket and extracted the small plastic bag that he always carried with him, and Henry dropped the piece of paper into the bag. Ken stared at the piece of paper, both sides were covered with print, the piece obviously torn out of a book. The paper was weathered, and the print was faded almost to the point of being indistinguishable.

Ken's heart nearly stopped, as he recognized a few of the words.

"Cursed is the man, who is hung on the tree."

CHAPTER 1 – DRESSING THE PART

K ristin Rosewood was ready. She stared at the mirror. The voice in her head whispered, "perfect".

She saw her head in the mirror nod in agreement. The black dress fit like a glove, and anyone who knew fashion, knew that this dress was created by someone who charged several normal people's annual wage for it. It's near transparent bodice and thigh high slit, left nothing to the imagination. It was practically scandalous. On Kristin, it would be the talk of the town, and accepted as appropriate. After all, it was on Kristin Rosewood.

For a forty-two-year-old woman, she looked barely over thirty. That was a good thing since her husband was five years her junior and was still the photogenic male he had been when she first met him. It had taken her three years of planning and effort to pry him loose from his wife and family, but she had been successful. He had divorced his wife, citing irreconcilable differences.

His first wife, Chris, had missed all the warning signs, as she had thought Kristin was a friend and advisor. It was Chris who had set up the meeting between Jim and Kristin, thinking it was simply her wealthy friend considering supporting her husband in the political race he was undertaking. She never figured out, that Kristin had arranged everything, down to making Chris think it was her own idea, not Kristin's. Kristin had used their supposed friendship to plan the attack. Her motto was simple, "If I can take it, you never really had it to start with".

Jim had been like putty in Kristin's hands, never catching on that the meetings, her suggestions, and finally that delicious night at the restaurant where Kristin deliberately drunk to much wine ensuring that Jim would drive her home, were all orchestrated to produce the desired result. Jim, a successful prosecutor, now looking to take on a more national role, was thrilled by his conquest of the woman who seemed to understand him better than his wife ever would. On top of that Kristin was rich and seemed to be his good luck charm. Every problem he faced, her mere presence seemed to result in a solution. She was also handling the funding of his campaign drive. He shed his wife of thirteen years and his three children, never believing that he had been anything but in control.

Of course, there had been the little matter of Kristin's own husband. Buddy House was an entrepreneur on his way to becoming a very wealthy man. For a farm boy, he had shed the entire small-town upbringing, and had built an astonishing empire of adult entertainment venues through several states. He had married Kristin not yet out of high school, when he learned that she was pregnant. Kristin's little black book of names and dates had been the start of Buddy's building of the financial empire that would fuel his own desire for power and meaning. He never learned that the pregnancy was not his doing. In fact, neither of their children were Buddy's offspring. Jim and Sue both came from the only failures in Kristin's otherwise faultless judgment. Kristin used Buddy's own ego and self-absorption to hide the truth about the origins of their children.

It was the father of Susan who had given Kristin the idea of how she would rid herself of Buddy, so she could marry Jim. Buddy's budding empire of strip joints was funded by two mysterious investors, who provided Buddy the ability to expand far beyond his own capabilities. But Buddy had run into trouble, and the investors had warned Kristin that Buddy might decide to reveal parts of their arrangement that they could not afford to have ever come to light.

That was in fact, exactly what Buddy had decided to do, revealing to Kristin both his financial plight, and his plan to turn state evidence against the two investors. That admission played right into Kristin's own plans. Kristin no longer needed Buddy's money, she was rich from her own activities. She also no longer needed Buddy's presence shielding her from scrutiny. She had someone who wanted her even more than Buddy, who was a rising political star and would provide an even more effective shield, without the negative attention that the Parlors were now bringing. It had been time for a change.

Buddy's temper and his known proclivity to violence, along with the fact that the FBI were on their way to spirit Buddy and Kristin away to a new life, provided the perfect cover for Kristin. When the FBI arrived at their home, they discovered a hysterical wife, and an almost dead Buddy House, waiting for them. Jim Rosewood, the successful prosecutor, arrived in time to ensure that Kristin's story of self-defense was the only logical outcome to the review of what had happened. Kristin's story was simple, she had told Buddy she was leaving him to marry someone else, and Buddy had gone crazy trying to stab her with the butcher's knife found lying close to Buddy's body.

The knife had Buddy's fingerprints clearly on it, and the gun Kristin had used to defend herself, was also Buddy's. Kristin had added that Buddy had been raving about the collapse of his empire while trying to kill her, adding another insight into the unglued mind of her now deceased husband. The facts all fit together nicely, exonerating her of any blame. She had been released into the protective care of Jim Rosewood, and the future had been sealed.

There had been a brief time of concern, when the paramedics had come and declared that Buddy was still alive. But that concern quickly ended when they had radioed that they had never made the hospital before he had died. There was no one alive that could dispute the facts as outlined by Kristin and supported by Jim.

Three years past and Jim was on his way to Washington DC, with his soon to be fiancé in tow. The wedding of Kristin Bloaden to freshman senator Jim Rosewood, was one of the media events in Washington DC. Jim Rosewood had risen quickly through the ranks of the senators in his party. He was bright, ambitious and he was married to Kristin.

Her striking figure matched with the shoulder length blond hair and sparkling green eyes turned many a man's head in Washington. What most of the men did not know, but soon discovered, her genus level IQ powered her cunning use of her beauty to devastating results. It was no accident, that Jim was suddenly offered positions in the leadership that would typically have taken far longer to reach. Kristin was like the bow of an icebreaker, clearing the path for Jim to reach the goals of his own ambition, only quicker. After the scandals that had rocked the Washington DC political elite, many suddenly realized that the price of their still undiscovered indiscretions was better paid to Kristin than taking the chance that their own careers would suddenly implode.

Jim's meteoric rise to power was noted by many. But his own brilliance, and drive, quickly dissuaded anyone from digging to deeply into the real reason for that rise. Tonight, would be the icing on the cake. Tonight, the world was about to learn, that the sitting President of the United States was picking a new Vice Presidential candidate to replace the man who had unexpectedly withdrawn his name from consideration for a second term. Kristin knew why the man had chosen to withdraw. She also knew who the new Vice-Presidential candidate would be, and Kristin realized what would come next, if everything went well over the next four years.

The image in the mirror smiled even more brightly. All the hard work had paid off. She would finally be the center of the power she had always wanted.

The voice reminded her, "They would be," and the image in the mirror nodded in agreement.

CHAPTER 2 – REMEMBERING THE PAST, FACING THE FUTURE

Ken turned off the road and drove up the short driveway that led to his two story farm house and pulled in front of the Quonset hut, that served as his repair shop. He and Bernice had settled on the small farm the same day he had discovered he was going to be a father. Bernice had wanted to live closer to her sister, and the farm was immediately adjacent to Bernice's family farm. For Ken, the six preceding years had been filled with change, especially with Bernice.

He had had a crush on Bernice from the time he was nine years old. She had come with her family to Ken's father's church, and Ken still remembered the first time she had agreed to go walking with Ken away from Sunday school. They had walked and talked and for three short years, until he was thirteen, they had been friends. Well, maybe more than friends, as he had tried to place his first sloppy kiss on Bernice when he was only ten. But something had changed when he had turned thirteen, about the same time he had been admitted to the membership at the church. Something new in his life was driving Bernice away, and despite his desire to continue in the relationship with Bernice, it became evident that was not to be.

For five years he had watched Bernice from a distance, still longing for a return of the old familiarity, yet her sights appeared to be on far different goals. Ken knew she had dated widely after they had stopped being a couple. He thought they were still friends, but even that seemed to wane as the years passed, and soon Bernice hardly appeared to notice when he was present. She had stopped coming to church within a couple of years of their breakup, and Ken only saw her occasionally either at school, or in town.

Bernice dropped out of school when she was a junior and started working at the local feed and hardware store when she was eighteen. Ken went away briefly to college, but returned to the town when he was twenty when his mother was diagnosed with cancer. She died quickly, leaving both Ken and Ken's father with a gaping hole in their lives. Abigail was the glue that held his father together, her and his father's faith that is. Ken determined that it would be better for his father to have him around, and the opening for a deputy working for the sheriff provided the perfect excuse for staying.

Ken moved back to the manse that was his father's home, that was immediately adjacent to the small country church his father had pastored for more than twenty five years. It was the only home Ken had ever known, and his father's vocation ensured that Ken learned much about the faith he now embraced.

It was ironic, that it was the Parlor that provided the money to allow the sheriff to hire Ken as the third deputy. Amazingly Ken discovered that he enjoyed the work, and before long even the sheriff realized that Ken was a natural heir to the sheriff's position. Devin Little, the sheriff who had hired Ken, had followed in his own father's footsteps, and was entering his fifth term as sheriff when Ken joined the force. It was the Parlor that brought Bernice back into Ken's life.

Bernice had always dreamt of moving away from Hitchenburgh. For her the world was a wondrous place, so much bigger and brighter than the sleepy little town. She had visited Kalamazoo, and Ken overheard her speaking of the wonders of that city, and wondering aloud about even larger cities. She was aware that her maturing physical beauty could provide her with much of the resources she would need to make such a change. Bernice had been turning men's heads from the time she was a sophomore in high school. Bernice had captured Ken's imagination far earlier, before she had matured into the beautiful woman she was becoming. There was a sparkle in her eyes, which Ken found irresistible.

The promise of more money than anyone had ever seen in the town, was not only the offer that had swayed the town council, but also the offer that lured many of the more attractive daughters of the town into the Parlor's orbit. The Parlor had existed for three years before the gravity of money had drawn Bernice.

Ken's father had fought tirelessly against the granting of the zoning that would allow the Parlor to be built. Ken remembered that it was one of the few times he had seen his father's faith shaken. His father could not accept that the presence of the Parlor would be permitted. What hurt his father even more was the final vote, and the final hand that was raised to permit the Parlor's existence. Ken's mother had died less than a year before that fateful vote, and that event along with the Parlor's zoning approval had driven his father, Pastor Jerry Farr, to the brink of despair.

It was also the event that funded the position that Ken had taken, to permit him to return home, to aid the man who had always been the strong tree that Ken had relied on. He had seen his father lose that strength becoming a bruised reed, easily to be broken. But events would show, that the truth never snapped what it had bruised.

Ken knew the story of the fight that Bernice had with Sally, Bernice's sister, the day she finally gave into the temptation. Buddy House was always looking for new talent, and with Bernice's looks, her arrival at the Parlor had guaranteed her a position. It was Sally's call that first day, when Bernice had failed to make it home from her job at the feed store by twelve PM, that had sent Ken out to search for her. He had found her green truck parked in the Parlor's lot and had watched as she exited the employee's door at two o'clock in the morning. His heart had dropped when he realized that Bernice was now working at the Parlor.

Ken was the night shift at the sheriff's office, and part of his routine was to arrive at the Parlor around one-thirty in the morning, to help any of the inebriated patrons make the correct decision to accept a ride to the local motel by the highway, or if they refused, to become guests of the town at the local poky. Sheriff's Little's policy was to provide free taxi service for the smart, or the soon to be DWI's an escorted ride to jail. Most accepted the ride to the motel.

However, that morning, two of the Parlor's patrons appeared to be especially inebriated, and Ken had watched torn between his desire to confront Bernice, and his responsibility to the two patrons. The confrontation with Bernice had been quick and straightforward. Sally's concern was relayed, and Bernice's petulant answer, which struck Ken as the response of a spoiled child, was soon relayed to Sally via the sheriff's car communication system. At least Bernice was physically safe, although Ken's heart was heavy with the sorrow that came from her decision to work at the Parlor.

7

Ken had quickly returned to his role as the protector of the town's patrons at the Parlor, and the two business men, declined the generous offer of a ride to the local motel. Instead, in their inebriated condition, they made the foolish choice that resulted in their joining the ranks of other visitors who now would face the wheels of justice.

What happened over the next few days changed everything for the town, and for Bernice and Ken. Within three days, the Parlor was gone, as were more than forty lives. Bernice had been spared from the destruction, just barely escaping the horrific events. It took two years after the events of that day, but Bernice had been drawn back to Ken's friendship and then finally to his warm embrace.

They married three years after the demise of the Parlor, and a year after she had embraced the faith that had first driven Bernice away from Ken as a teenager. Also, within a year of the wedding, Ken began his new role as sheriff of the town, after Sheriff Little retired, and with his backing, Ken was easily elected his replacement.

Ken turned off his car's engine and saw that the back door light came on. Bernice was waiting for him. He glanced at his watch. It was after eleven PM, an especially late evening for him. Bernice had opened the back door, and her smile reassured Ken, that everything was still okay on the home front.

"Long day?" Bernice said as Ken slid past her and into their home.

"Yes, it sure has been" Ken said.

He embraced Bernice and planted a kiss on her lips, much more deliberate and practiced than that first kiss so many years ago. His heart still fluttered when he realized that she was in his arms. Her sheer warmth flooding his soul and revitalizing his tired mind.

"Kids okay?" Ken's normal question.

Bernice had turned aside to give him room to enter the house.

"Yes, missing their daddy tucking them in, and telling them the story about the angels, but yes they are fine" Bernice said.

Ken stopped.

The mention of angels returning his mind to the present and the day that had just past and the day he knew he was facing tomorrow. Bernice felt the change in his body and looked at him

"They're back?" Bernice asked, her voice not concealing her concern.

All Ken could do was nod.

CHAPTER 3 – RETURNING VISITORS

After the discovery of the cause of the death of the tree, and the extra revelation that someone had visited the tree recently and posted yet another cryptic note, Ken had left the site to keep an eleven-thirty appointment with his father. Before he left he asked Henry to keep the discoveries confidential. Henry had readily agreed and seemed as relieved to be leaving the tree as Ken was.

Ken had just enough time to stop at the station, before he would do the easy walk over to the home where his father now resided. Jerry Farr, Ken's father, had left the manse and his pastorate when he turned seventy. He had spent more than thirty-five years working among his flock, and the events surrounding the rise and fall of the Hitchenburgh Parlor seemed to have swirled around his final years as Grace Presbyterian's pastor. The fact that another of the survivors of the demise of the Parlor was now the new pastor at Grace, seemed more than appropriate. Ken knew it had been his father's recommendation that had resulted in the call to the newly minted pastor.

His father's selflessness never ceased to amaze Ken. Having worked all those years, his father stepped aside just as the church finally appeared to be growing, passing the three hundred mark for the first time. Ken was constantly amazed of the number of lives the demise of the Parlor had touched. The new pastor arrived, with his pregnant wife beside him.

The new pastor was a former marine, and an FBI plant into Buddy House's growing empire. He had been sent to work as a bouncer at the Hitchenburgh Parlor to protect another FBI agent who had infiltrated even further into the organization. The destruction of the Parlor had rendered the new pastor blind, but he had managed to protect the other agent, who was now his wife. Together they had moved into the manse, leaving the question of where Ken's father was going to live unanswered.

Ken and Bernice had invited his father to come stay with them, in their new home, but Ken realized that their announcement of the pending addition to their family probably was a factor in his father declining the offer. Instead his father accepted another offer, and now resided in the town in a home that still belonged to Buddy House's half-brother. The house had been left to Glenn Hitch by their mother when she had died, less than a week before Pastor Jerry's last service at Grace.

Pastor Jerry had officiated at the service for Emma House, and in retrospect it was appropriate that service was the last service his father had to conduct at Grace. But that had not meant that his father had really retired. His move to the house just off Main Street in town meant that his father could easily walk to the large First Presbyterian Church that anchored the main street of Hitchenburgh. As fate would have it, or as both Jerry and Ken believed, providence, the pastor at First Presbyterian also was a victim of the demise of the Parlor. Although in his case, he was still very much alive.

It was his hand, which had been raised at that fateful council meeting, the final and deciding vote allowing the building of the first of Buddy House's Parlors. Within a year of the demise of the Parlor, Pastor Kevin Hill had left his wife Faith, and his three children and run away with Alison Day, the daughter of one of the elders of the church. It had been that event that brought the session of First Presbyterian to Ken's father, and their request that he help them through the process of figuring out what they were supposed to do.

Pastor Farr had been working with the session for more than four years now. Never officially being called as the pastor of the church but residing over the church activities while the session continued to struggle through the shock waves left behind by the departure of Kevin Hill. The church was looking for a replacement pastor, but until one was found, Ken's father was the semi-permanent pulpit supply that was needed.

Ken's father continued to preach, and under the circumstances had taken on most of the responsibilities of a full-time pastor. Among his responsibilities was reaching out to Kevin Hill and to Alison Day, hoping and praying that something he might say or do would bring back the wayward couple. With news of Kevin's divorce being finalized over the objections of his first wife Faith and the additional information of Kevin's intention to marry Alison, Ken's father had started the process that would eventually lead both to the defrocking of Kevin and to his excommunication from the church.

That was when things had really gotten interesting, as Kevin had no intention of simply vanishing off the stage the pulpit had been for him. Instead he had chosen to fight the charges both within the church governmental structure, and when that had failed, to find a way to bring the events into the civil litigation process. The result was that Kevin had lost his church case but won his civil case. His argument before the court was that the actions of the church were a direct infringement on his personal liberties; libelous in their accusations and that the church had no intrinsic right to deny him his ability to make a living in his chosen profession. Of even more interest was the fact that a church in Connecticut had hired Kevin and was supporting him in his battle with this former denomination, church, and most particularly with Pastor Jerry Farr.

Once again Ken's father was in the middle of a battle, but this time one that appeared less spiritual and more civil. The damages awarded to Kevin by the first court were enough to take ones breathe away. There had been no doubt, the fight would continue, and both the denomination, and the local church, appealed the lower court decision to the next higher court. That decision to appeal had not come lightly, as Ken's father was convinced that fighting a spiritual battle in an earthly court was unwise. Despite the civil nature of the arguments, Ken's father remained convinced that spiritual forces, far above the human judges presiding over the case, were involved. He had been persuaded not to stand in the way of the local church or the denomination in their appeal. Both saw the award as an erosion of the protections that religion was afforded under the constitution.

The decision of the state high court was due on Wednesday, and Ken's father would be spending Tuesday fasting and praying about the outcome. Ken's father never mentioned the civil judgment the lower court had rendered against him. The two-million-dollar award was three times more money than his father had made in all of the time he had worked at Grace. Ken remembered the jubilant Kevin Hill's proclamation that "justice had been served." If that was justice, Ken wanted nothing to do with it. Ken was happy the denomination and church were appealing the award, even if his father wasn't.

Ken's appointment with his father had three goals. First to make sure he ate something, as he had the tendency to forget to eat, and then go straight into a day of fasting. Secondly, Ken needed to know his father was holding up under all the stress. And finally, for the last three years his father had been his sounding board about Ken's thoughts about the troubling case of the death of Hastings Moment. Ken would talk through the evidence with his father, and then look for his guidance. Often, that guidance was an hour in prayer, but Ken had discovered that clarity seemed to come during those periods more than any other time.

Ken parked the car at the sheriff's station, little more than a store front on Main Street about two blocks from the large First Presbyterian Church. The station still had only three desks, two less than what would be needed if all of the deputies were in at the same time. But the staggered nature of the hours made sure that for the most part the tight quarters were never unmanageable. On top of that, the station had two holding cells. Both cells had been vacant for months, will little need of them since the demise of the Parlor. Before that event the cells often would hold the inebriated patrons of the Parlor who had refused the offer of a ride to the local motel.

When Ken entered the station he saw that both deputies, Dan Doodle and David White, were watching something on the small television they maintained in the station. Ken saw the President of the United States on the screen, and he stopped to watch and listen as well. The president was announcing his new running mate for the upcoming election and at the mention of Senator Jim Rosewood, the audience on the television erupted in applause.

"See her, there she is!" Dan said to David.

"Look what she is wearing, it hides almost nothing!" David said in response.

Then Dan had pushed a few buttons, the picture had backed up, and the whole announcement repeated. Ken realized that they were watching something that had been recorded and were replaying a segment to confirm what they thought they had seen.

Ken watched as they froze the screen, and sure enough, there was Kristin Bloaden, now Rosewood, her trademark hair and bosom on display for the whole world to see. The dress she was wearing was a sheer black one piece, that fit her like a second skin, and even on the television screen there was no doubt about the curves it barely concealed.

"She's still as beautiful as she was back in high school," Dan said.

"Yeah, and she still makes sure you know it," replied Dan.

"So, this is what the tax payers pay you for," Ken said, suddenly getting the previously distracted deputies' attention.

"You can leave it on, as I haven't seen this. When is this from?" Ken asked the two flustered deputies.

"Last night, the President announced that Jim Rosewood was going to be his running mate, and of course that means that one of Hitchenburgh's own is sitting right next to the man, who might one day be President of the United States!" Dan replied as a way of introduction.

The tape continued to play on, the announcement followed by remarks by the new vice-presidential candidate thanking both the President and the party for their confidence in him. Jim Rosewood sure sounded sincere, as he continued the short speech where he promised to fulfill this calling with the same intensity and focus that had become his trademark in the Senate. Then there was a short question and answer period for the President and the new Vice Presidential candidate. All the while Kristin Rosewood's smiling face shone just slightly behind her husband. One thing was for sure, whenever Kristin moved, the camera seemed to follow her. Ken was convinced that the camera man must have been as awe struck as were the two deputies. It was as if the president and potential vice president were not even there.

Finally a female reporters' voice had sounded a question. Ken knew that voice, although the camera never left its focus to show the reporter asking the question.

"Kristin what do you think of your husband decision to run for the Vice Presidential spot?" asked the voice.

That caused both the President and Jim Rosewood to turn in Kristin's direction, giving the cameraman an even clearer shot of Kristin. The question seemed so out of place, and it was then that Ken realized the President's wife was nowhere to be seen on the stage.

'Kristin's face and figure seemed to momentarily fill the screen.

"I'm thrilled for Jim, and I am sure that he will make an excellent Vice President" Kristin said.

All the time she was speaking, even for this short statement, the camera was focusing in on her, and the camera appeared to slowly descend making sure that the whole package was on display.

"Whoever the cameraman is, he's going to lose his job when his bosses see this footage," Dan exclaimed.

"It's almost pornographic in its focus on her attributes," David said nodding in agreement.

Ken just continued to watch without comment on his two deputies' thoughts.

The voice asked a second question.

"What does it feel like to know that you are so close to being our number one again?" the voice asked.

It had been the same female voice but had taken on strange gravelly tone as the question was asked. Ken felt every muscle in his body tense, as he watched Kristin and the brief emotional ripple that rolled across her face.

"You mean, how does it feel, to know that Jim might be called upon at some point to lead this great country of ours?", Kristin had responded almost immediately, as if that had really been the question.

Kristin did not wait for a response from the voice.

"Well, every person that accepts the role of Vice President knows that they may someday need to fulfill that need, if it ever arises, but like the current Vice President, our hopes are always that the need never occurs, but if it occurs, Jim will have my full support and encouragement. But I think this is a good time to salute the man who has decided not to run for another term, and who has been a whole hearted supporter of my husband for this role" and with that introduction the current Vice President appeared on the screen next to Kristin and then Kristin had slowly faded into the background.

Another minute of a speech by the soon to be former Vice President, his resounding support for Jim Rosewood announced, two more questions, and the tape was done.

"Well that's it," said Dan, pushing the button that turned off and ejected the tape.

"Do you mind Dan, if I could have that tape? I'll give it back to you tomorrow," Ken asked.

"Sure, you can have it!" Dan said. His eyebrows raised in questioning surprise.

Ken accepted the tape, and then said.

"Guys, anything I need to know?"

Neither man answered both just shaking their heads negatively.

"Good, I'll be back around one, I am going over to my dad's for lunch to see how he's doing," Ken said.

Taking the tape Ken exited the office and did the two block walk to his fathers' home.

The two-story Victorian home sat just off the road. There was no drive way, so parking was always on the street. The street in front of his fathers' house was normally empty but today his father's car, an old Buick Century already over twenty years old, was flanked by Jenny Housher's car and a third car, a large black Chevy Suburban sat immediately behind Jenny's car. Jenny had been Emma House's closest friend, so the presence of her car did not surprise Ken. It was that third vehicle that surprised him as it looked like a government vehicle, the type you always saw in the TV shows. Ken walked up the steps to the house and knocked on the door.

His father opened the door almost immediately.

"Come on in Ken," his father said.

His father was just under six foot tall, and thin, but still ramrod straight. His hair was now totally white, and over the past two years he had developed a full face of wrinkles, that announced his increasing age. Yet his voice was still strong, and he still walked like a man much younger in age.

Ken entered the home, the door opening directly into the small kitchen that took up about a third of the downstairs floor. Seated in the kitchen were Jenny Housher, and three men Ken did not recognize. Standing next to the sink was Glenn Hitch, his hand still holding his trademark staff. Ken stopped, taking in the scene. The presence of Glenn, who had not been back to Hitchenburgh in over two years, told Ken something was up. He nodded at Glenn and greeted Jenny.

"Ken, this is Agent Larry Smithers and this is Agent Doug Brooks of the FBI, they are two of Glenn's friends, and they came over to speak with Jenny," his father said as an introduction. Ken shook both men's offered hands. Ken turned to the final man who had been seated with his back to Ken. That man stood and turned, facing Ken.

He was much thinner than what Ken remembered, and the bluster that had seemed to radiate from the man before was gone. His eyes no longer had that manic shine that Ken had read as a cross between brilliance and downright craziness.

Ken realized that he was raising his left hand to offer to shake, his right hand and arm seemed unable to move. Ken could not believe he was seeing who he was seeing. His father had just begun to say,

"Ken, I think you know…"

His father never got to complete the introduction, as Ken blurted, "Your dead!"

The man face contorted slightly but then a smile broke through, that was neither manic nor upset. Instead the smile seemed to communicate acceptance of events beyond his own control.

"As my brother said, the first time he met me when he came home, "Apparently Not"".

Ken finally took the man's offered hand awkwardly, unsure about shaking left hand to left hand and shook Buddy House's hand.

CHARLES DE ANDRADE

CHAPTER 4 – KRISTIN

The ride back to their Arlington, VA home from the press conference where her husband was introduced as the new vice-presidential candidate was not the basking in success memory that Kristin had expected. Instead she spent most of the drive reliving the unexpected confrontation. What she had planned for was a coming out event and instead she had been sidelined by that ghastly reporters' question that had sent her scurrying away from the center of attention. She had been totally unprepared for the question that had resurfaced a memory she thought was long buried.

Equally troubling was the complete silence of the voice that had been her constant companion and advisor for years. She recognized the voice, but it had come from that reporter. Why had the voice left her and seemingly joined with the reporter?

Kristin complemented herself on her rapid, unassisted recovery. The question asked had been so odd, she was certain many other reporters would have at least said "huh?" Apparently, her rapid recovery and covering diversionary translation of the question, had satisfied the crowd. Kristin though was anything but satisfied.

She remembered the reporter, having seen her at another gathering she had attended almost three years ago, but she did not remember her name. She made a mental note to remedy that problem quickly. She needed to know, how that reporter had stumbled onto that long-hidden secret. As far as Kristin knew, only four people on earth knew about the event, that the reporter had alluded to, and two of them were dead, and the third would not dare share anything about the event as it would mean his destruction as well. The fourth person was herself. She thought about it a bit longer, and then realization hit her. Perhaps there was a fifth?

Jim had not seemed to notice his wife's distraction, and certainly had said nothing about the strange question. Instead he was bubbling all over himself about the opportunity he had just been given. Kristin had been listening, but her mind was busy unwrapping the more pressing problem.

"You know, the old man could not take his eyes off you even for a moment. Good thing his wife was not there. There was no question what was running through his mind!", Jim said.

That comment grabbed Kristin's attention back. Jim was chuckling and patting her exposed leg, just about as far up as he could go without giving the driver of the limo a heart attack.

She laughed. This was a game she and Jim had learned to play very effectively. Jim understood exactly the sensation Kristin had created, and he knew exactly the benefits that could come from her calculated performance. They had played this so many times, at so many dinners, and other social gatherings, it was almost second nature to both. Most husbands would have been upset by her behavior, but Jim was not like most husbands. He enjoyed the game, enjoyed the chase, and had even given her the go ahead to close the deal with any number of potential advisories and supporters. Kristin's electronic black book, recording each of the favors done, had served both Kristin and Jim very well. In fact, it was one of those favors, which had resulted in the early retirement of the current Vice President in favor of her husband.

Her husband also knew something else. Kristin had made it very clear to Jim, that if she ever caught him with any other woman, she would bury him alive with the scandal. Jim had accepted that arrangement without question, and the reality was, she was still incredible in bed. Jim accepted the one way only nature of the demanded fidelity. She was after all doing him the favor. She never took on anyone, her husband had not already agreed to as a target with benefit for himself.

Jim laughed again.

Kristin hit the button that raised the blackened window, sealing off the back of the car from the driver. For all practical purposes, they were alone now, and Jim's hand traveled further up her leg. Kristin laid back enjoying the sensation and allowing the troubling event to disappear from her mind.

"Yep, my dear, you better be careful, or that old man might just have a heart attack before the next election. We both know, we need to get past the next election before anything unfortunate happens," Jim said. Kristin just nodded, giving in to both her desire and her husband's.

When they got to the home, she straightened her dress before the driver opened the door. Together arm in arm, she and Jim strolled the short distance from the car to their residence. The door man opened the door, almost saluting Jim, as Kristin was sure he knew that he was holding the door for the next Vice President of the United States. The secret service car had followed the limo all the way home, and already the six agents assigned to Jim and Kristin were acting as if, Jim was the Vice President. They followed Jim and Kristin right into the lobby and into the elevator that took them to the top floor.

The residence that was the penthouse suite occupied the entire top floor of the six-story apartment building just east of the Pentagon in Crystal City. Kristin had bought the suite the year they first arrived in Washington, before they were even officially married. The suite was over six thousand feet of glorious extravagance. They often entertained guests at the residence and there were even five guest bedrooms available should some of their guests need to stay overnight. The agents would not be staying with them. Fortunately, a suite several floors down was available for rent, and Uncle Sam was picking up the tab. Two of the agents would always be posted by the elevator on the top floor. Kristin already liked the attention and knew this was only the beginning.

The agents already had the floor plans for their residence, but they had insisted at a firsthand viewing. They had said practically nothing as they did their survey. The senior agent in charge, a Mr. Smith, a stiff looking man of about forty, seeming immune to Kristin's glances, said, "Mr. Rosewood, two of our group will always be outside your door. As we said earlier, it is best that you always clear any excursions with us, before either you or your wife leave. We will have your complete daily itinerary on hand every morning from your chief of staff, and should you need to change anything just let us know."

With that he had left with the other agents in tow.

Jim swatted Kristin's rear as the door to the suite closed.

"Want a drink? I sure need one" he said, heading for the bar off the kitchen.

"Sure, just make mine a double of whatever you are having" she said laughing.

Kristin headed for the living room, stopping at the credenza by the front door, where her assistant would leave any mail that she thought either she, or Jim needed to see. There were three pieces of mail. She picked up the first piece, a squarish shaped invitation addressed to "Mrs. Kristin Rosewood. She saw the college emblem on it, a "Covenant College" on Lookout Mountain in Tennessee, and she opened it.

It was an invitation to her son's graduation. Amazingly, it included an announcement that her son would be giving the valedictorian address for the class, and that special seats for her, and one other person were reserved in the closest row to the front of the stage. She was shocked, suddenly realizing that she had not known that he was doing that well in college.

She had given up her children's care to her parents, after Buddy's death some five years ago. She paid for his college, but other than a few trips to visit her parents and her children over the holiday's she had not really been a part of their lives. They were from a different past, something that she had consciously left behind. Was it really five years?

Included in the card was a hand-written note from her son.

"Mom, I know that you have been incredibly busy, and the word is that Jim is about to be named to something important. The secret service arrived here two weeks ago, and they sort of alerted me to what was happening. I am just hoping that you might be able to attend my graduation, and to see Susan as well. You know, she is also graduating from her high school as the valedictorian as well on the next Saturday. I know she probably won't send you an invitation, as she doesn't think you would come anyway, but you really should. We both miss you terribly, and if you can only come to one, go to hers. She is so much like you, and she has worked so hard, you would be so proud of her. Hope to see you soon. Love, your son Jim."

His words touched her heart. It was so like him. Even as a youngster, in her darkest hours, he had always thought about his mother and his sister before himself. He was so like his father. That thought stopped her cold in her tracks. She wasn't going down that memory lane. She laid the invitation aside picking up the next envelop.

It was an official looking envelope with the IRS stamp and returned addresses clearly machine printed, and the evidence that the letter had been delivered by registered mail. She opened it and scanned its contents. Once again, they were auditing her returns. What a fishing trip, she fumed. They just never quit. Every year for the past five years they had demanded an audit, and every year her CPA and Tax Attorney had successfully defended her filings.

Fortunately, neither her accountants or the IRS were aware of the off- shore accounts. The accountants were able to argue with full confidence that Kristin Rosewood was a fine upstanding American always paying all the taxes that were due. In Kristin's view, the four to five million she paid every year in taxes was already more than she thought anyone should have to pay. She and Jim had even survived the incredible vetting they had to go through before the President named Jim as his running mate. Certainly, if they could not find any issues during the vetting, the IRS should finally give up on thinking they were going to discover anything in these ridiculous audits. She plopped that letter down, with the mental note to call the CPA and Tax Attorney in the morning and get the whole process started again.

Finally, only the last envelope waited. She scanned the return address and stopped cold.

Opening the envelope, she scanned the single sheet of paper, with precious few words written, in a scrawl she remembered well.

"Our daughter is seventeen. I understand she has turned into quite a fine specimen. We paid you well, and the deal was, when she was thirteen, she was mine. That was four years ago. It is time for you to fulfill your part of the deal. Avery."

That sent Kristin's mind running down memory lane, and this time, no manner of will power could stop her mind's racing. She did not hear Jim's voice, or feel the shot glass filled with her ordered double that he slid into her hand.

CHAPTER 5 – BUDDY

66They tell me that the second shot, the one that was meant to kill me, actually saved my life. The first shot severed both the artery and the main nerve to my arm. If the second shot had not stopped my heart, I would have bled out."

Agent Smithers interrupted the speaker, nodding as he said:

"When we got to Buddy's home there was so much blood under him, we were sure he was already gone. I felt his neck artery, there was no pulse. It wasn't until the paramedics arrived that one of them discovered he was still alive. We rushed him out of the house and towards the hospital. The paramedics kept working on him, and they were pumping fluids into him at an amazing rate. They managed to close off the artery, to keep Buddy from bleeding more. Their battlefield training had prepared them in ways that I still account as part of what saved him.

Even with all of their work, they kept warning me that he was weakening, and they were not sure he would survive the trip to the hospital. It was during the drive that it dawned on me that the brothers had to be involved in this and that if they discovered Buddy was still alive, they would come after him again. I had one of the paramedics make the call to his home, alerting everyone there that Buddy was officially dead.

I made a couple of other calls, and when we got to the hospital in Wilmington, everything was ready. Fortunately, there were two other shootings the same day. One of the other victims had died from his wounds. We managed to swap names, and suddenly Buddy was Robert Blaneshire. Buddy had already signed the papers to enter the witness protection program. It was obvious his wife wasn't going to join him. We had quite a discussion in the bureau afterwards as to whether I had done the right thing. Especially since it appeared that Buddy had tried to kill his wife. But, in the end, that story just didn't feel right, but it would take us some time before we could know for sure whether I had guessed right."

The man nodded and continued his story.

"Of course, nobody counted on me being in a coma for nine months. Apparently, I really am fortunate to be here today. When I finally woke up, it took another six months before I was able to walk, and even longer for me to regain my speech. The loss of blood was almost like a reverse stroke, my brain was starved for oxygen and that caused me to have many of the same symptoms of a stroke."

Ken had been listening but finally had to interrupt to ask his question. "How is it that the second shot didn't kill you? We were told it was a shot right to your heart," he asked.

The man's eyes were burning bright, and he turned slightly, looking at his brother.

"My brother saved me" hesitating and then completing his final word, "twice" he said.

He continued, "My brother visited me less than 24 hours before I was shot. He gave me something saying I needed to wear it, and he told me that I was going to be shot. I thought he was crazy, but so much was happening that I did not understand, that I stopped just before I got home, and put the vest on underneath my shirt. I didn't really think about it, just decided that it couldn't hurt. I'm not going to tell you I believed him, it was more of a rabbits' foot to me, a 'what if' than what it became. If I hadn't put it on, or if it had been a head shot…, his voice trailed off.

Silence reigned for several moments. The doorbell broke the silence. Ken watched as his father went again to the door, opening it.

"Come on in John. Chi how are you?" his fathers' words identifying who was at the door.

Ken watched as John Housher and his wife came in. John was truly a wall of a man. He was nearly six feet tall, but his girth was twice what Ken's was. Even now, six years after the demise of the Parlor, and almost ten years after his stint in the Marines ended, he was in incredible physical shape. John was the marine, the plant that had saved the woman who was now his wife. Chi had been the deep FBI agent inserted to find the evidence needed to prove what Buddy House had been up to. She had masqueraded as a dancer, shedding her clothes like a professional, and her skill and willingness to play the role, brought her into the inner sanctum of Buddy's blossoming kingdom.

Neither John nor Chi had discovered the evidence they were so desperately looking for.

But they had discovered one another. The destruction of the Parlor had blinded John, but the same event had brought John into the light and Chi into his arms. Ken had often heard him singing the John Newton hymn, and the words, "I was blind but now I see," were some of his favorites.

Ken marveled at the providence that had saved this man, and that this man had replaced his father at the church his father had pastored for over thirty-five years.

Next to him was his wife, Chi. She was petite in size, with rich dark black hair sliding down past her shoulders. Her sparkling brown eyes bracketed a thin and sharply defining nose, but it was her lips that attracted you immediately, they were full and sensuous. She was muscularly, and her body had the appearance of someone who took the effort to stay fit. Ken could see immediately that she would have been quite an attraction at the Parlor.

Ken also knew that she was the daughter of a local Hitchenburgh family. Her parents had been killed in a freak tornado accident, and she had been raised by her older brother Scott, who continued to farm the land he inherited from his parents. Chi and John had two children, Grace and Charity, and they were expecting their third child any day now. Together the family of four, soon to be five, were embedded in the community, and John's ministry was increasing in size and impact.

"Pastor, thank you for calling me. I'm not sure I can help, but I will certainly try, if I can," John said to Ken's father.

Ken saw Chi stop, placing her hand on John's arm. She had seen the man sitting on the dining room chair. Her jaw had dropped open, but no words came from her mouth, but John instinctively knew that something was wrong.

'What's wrong, Chi?," John's tone instantly communicating his awareness of a problem.

The man got up from his chair and walked slowly towards John and Chi, and then did something totally unexpected; he knelt in front of John. "Hi John," his voice strong, but the tone also wary.

Ken saw John's knees bend, the shock of the voice like a body blow to the standing man that towered over the man on his knees.

"Buddy?", John's single word, more confirmation than question.

"Yes, John, it's me. I have so much to ask your and Chi's forgiveness for, and your mom as well. I asked the pastor if it would be possible for you to be here today as well," the knelling man said bursting into tears at the same time.

John reached down, feeling the shoulder of the man. For an instance Ken was afraid that he was going to snap the neck of his onetime friend. Ken saw the same fear flash through Jenny Housher's eyes, as well. John certainly had every reason to, for it was this man that had driven John's father to kill himself. It was this man, who had used everyone, even his own friends and family, to get what he wanted for himself. Ken knew that John hated everything Buddy House had built and become.

But then John had folded to his knees as well, and while still towering over the much smaller Buddy had wrapped his arms around the weeping man and consoled him like a father would an injured child. Ken realized now, for the first time, why his father had willingly recommended John as his replacement. Like his father, John was a pastor in the deepest recesses of his being. Later when everyone had moved to the living room, and the discussion had continued, Jenny Housher finally asked a question.

"Why didn't you come home when your mother was dying Buddy?

She died not knowing you were alive," Jenny's assertion both a genuine question and accusation at the same time.

"It has taken me a long time, to come to terms with everything I have done, especially to my mom. You are probably the best person to understand why I did not come home before. I just could not admit to myself, much less my mother, that I had been responsible for my father's death," Buddy said.

Ken felt the weight in the air. He knew from Buddy's voice, that he had finally admitted something, that he had probably never voiced before. Then

Buddy said something that made that fact crystal clear:

"I killed my father. I pushed him on the steps on Christmas eve all those years ago, and he fell backwards and broke his neck. It wasn't an accident, I did it deliberately. It's the one thing I've done, that despite everything my brother has said, and the pastor has said, I still have a hard time believing, I can be forgiven for. I've only started to believe that I have been forgiven for everything else, but that act…"

Once again, Buddy had choked up.

Agent Smither's picked up again, while Buddy tried to regain his composure. The agent looked directly at Jenny.

"When Buddy was finally able to communicate, he told us that you and his mom had all of his papers. That is why we contacted you four years ago asking about the papers. Fortunately, you didn't force us to tell you how we knew you had them. We've spent the last four years unraveling everything and we finally have put together enough evidence to make our move against the brothers. Of course, Hastings was killed before we could take him in, but Avery has continued the business, and we discovered Avery has some very interesting partners that replaced his brother in his business, and that is why we are here today. We wanted to warn everyone what's about to happen."

"I won't testify against her," Buddy said, his voice finally returning.

Agent Smither's nodded, the action hinting that this had been an ongoing discussion between Buddy and the FBI special agent.

Ken understood exactly who the "her "was.

The doorbell again, interrupted, and this time Ken got up and went to the door and opened it. Outside stood two young adults. He recognized both, but the young man had grown at least another six inches since he had gone away to college, and he had filled out into a handsome man. His sandy hair was swept back from his forehead, and his brown eyes radiated both intelligence and warmth. The younger woman was the man's sister. She too had blossomed into a wonderfully beautiful woman. Her blond hair spoke of her mother, but her almond color skin matched neither her mother nor her fathers, and her eyes were greenish gray in their hue, again not a shared trait. She too radiated intelligence and her smile was just as bright and delightful as her brothers'.

"Come on in Jim and Susan, glad you were able to make it!" Ken said, stepping aside to let them in.

The living room was open to the kitchen, and both Jim and Susan moved instinctively for the living room, since that was where everyone was. There were two additional chairs that were empty, obviously set up for their arrival.

Ken felt the tension in the room elevate as they entered. Neither sat down, both just stood staring at the man sitting next to Glenn on the sofa. Slowly Buddy had stood, walking unsteadily towards the two young people.

"Dad?" Ken heard Jim say first.

Then an intense sob echoed in the room, and everyone turned to look at Jenny Housher, who had broken down and was weeping.

CHAPTER 6 – AVERY

Kristin rocked back and forth rhythmically, and Jim's groaning increased matching her own increasing excitement. When it was over, Kristin disengaged from Jim, rolling over.

"God, Kristin, you just keep getting better!" Jim exclaimed.

Kristin smiled. This was one of the reasons she liked Jim, he was so easily pleased.

Kristin realized that Jim had been completely unaware of how distant she really had been, her mind racing, covering over and over the problems she was facing, and the potential solutions. She had used the time with Jim, almost as a time out, where she could release some of the tensions freeing her mind to consider the problems. She had outlined each of the problems and proposed to herself the different potential solutions. Her most pressing problem was what to do about Avery Moment's demands.

Her solutions had been whittled down to four: kill him, give him what he wanted, turn him in to the authorities or give him something he wanted even more. She discarded the third one, as that would expose her own complicity in what Avery had been doing, and finally she focused in on the last solution. She had something Avery wanted even more. In fact, she knew he was sorely lacking in that asset, as he was not near the businessman his brother had been.

Kristin also knew that his desire for Susan had little to do with Susan, and everything to do with what his brother had done to him. Kristin recalled the bargain with his brother and smiled at the thought of the demise of the seemingly successful partnership between the two brothers, Kristin replacing Avery as his brother's business partner. Of course, there had been the other demand as well. Avery was less than half the man he used to be, if you could even call him a man anymore.

After Hastings had been murdered, something that Kristin had not foreseen or participated in, she had been forced to hide her ownership in Hastings's enterprises even further. Fortunately, Hastings had done an excellent job of hiding both of their involvements in the various endeavors that had made them both exceedingly rich. Kristin remembered that she had prepared for the eventuality that she would need to shed any connection to the Parlors, or their replacements, the ever-expanding chain now called Revelations.

Jim never asked where her money came from and Kristin certainly did not divulge that information to anyone. She had managed to funnel off, a decent size chunk of the funds into other more respectable businesses, which for the world, was the visible source of her success and wealth.

When Hastings died one of the loose ends that Kristin had tied up had to do with Avery. She remembered chiding herself for the document she had inserted into a whole series of documents that Avery had to sign and date, fearful that he would discover what her backup plan was. She had gambled that Avery would not read what it was he was signing, and he hadn't. His hatred towards both his brother and Kristin had so clouded his judgment, that he had signed everything that day in the lawyer's office, without benefit of explanation as to what it was, he was signing. Each document had been notarized, forever embedding the evidence of the age of the documents. Kristin had slipped the document back out of the set, before the rest had been filed with the government, but not before the attorney and the accountant had made copies for their files. To this day, that original document resided in her safe in her office and only she knew of its existence. It was time for the document to see the light of day. It would give Avery what he did not know, he already had.

Kristin smiled to herself. It was a good plan. It dealt with two of the problems, Avery's demands, and the increasingly determined IRS audits at the same time.

She rolled back on to Jim, straddling his midsection with her thighs. In several short minutes, they were both well on their way to another climax, and this time, she was not distracted.

In the morning, Kristin had rolled out of bed, being sure not to disturb her soundly sleeping husband. She knew the car would be waiting as her daily visit to the local gym that catered to the wealthy and important people in

Washington DC. She knew that visit would certainly be on the list of activities the Secret Service had down as a regular occurrence.

She made the bathroom, sliding the door closed, and pulled out her cell phone. The two calls had gone as well as they could have. The one with Avery, short and to the point, the meeting place and time set. The other, went even better.

She slipped through the bedroom, Jim was still asleep, and into her office, sliding that door closed as well. She found the safe, dialed in the combination, and removed the document, folding it and putting it into a business envelop. Her final step took longer than she intended, and it almost changed her plan. Sitting at the computer she had accessed the ten different overseas banks, and made the transfers, consolidating everything into one account, at the one bank mentioned in the document. She then closed all of the other accounts, and using each bank's new security systems, ended any trace of those accounts existence. The US governments' insistence for access to foreign banks previously secret accounts had born some fruit, but the banks had created new security systems allowing clients to destroy the evidence without the banks taking any action on their own. They truly could plead ignorance and innocence at the same time.

It was when Kristin viewed the newly combined account that her only doubt about her plan arose. She stared at the balance, hardly believing what she was seeing. She knew the different investments had paid off, but she never thought of herself as a billionaire, before today. It took her reviewing her options again, before she made up her mind. She would still be rich, even without the 1.2 billion that now sat in the combined account. She turned the computer off heading back to the bathroom.

After a quick shower she packed her gym bag with the items she would need, to make her escape from the new security that now surrounded both her and her soon to be Vice Presidential husband. She put on the one- piece body stocking, choosing to forgo both her bra and her panties. She needed to distract the secret service agents, and if it wasn't the senior agent, who appeared oblivious to her wiles, she was sure this would do the trick. Putting her shoulder length hair into a pony tail, she made sure that anything she could prepare for her escape ahead of time was done.

She threw on her long jacket, hiding her planning, for the walk to the elevator, and down to the car. Sure enough, a young secret service agent was waiting just outside her door. He followed her to the elevator, and accompanied her down to the ground floor, where another agent joined them as well. Together they headed towards the limousine that waited for Kristin for the ride to the gym. One of the agents opened the limo door for her, and that is when she removed her jacket throwing it into the car, and then slid seductively into place onto the seat.

Kristin had seen the eyes of both agents. They had seen everything she wanted them to see. The door to the car had stood open at least ten seconds longer than it should have, before the one agent finally closed it. Kristin watched as the two men stood stunned outside her car.

"Let's get going," Kristin snapped at her driver.

The driver obeyed, not waiting for the two agents to get to their own car.

Kristin punched the button, bringing the window up between her and the driver. She had hired Earl, a sixty something black man, who had been driving taxis most of his life. He had impressed her with his driving skills on a trip to New York. She offered him the job making five times what he made every year as a taxi cab driver. It really had been a no brainer for Earl. She had seen Earl's eyes racking her body with the appreciative stares. Last thing she needed now was for an accident. She slipped back into her jacket.

Kristin watched as the two agents hurried back to their waiting car. She would have loved to hear their conversation once they made their own car. But Kristin had gotten the jump on them, and it would buy her the minutes she needed for her plan. By the time the agents would make the gym, Kristin would already be inside. Before they could deploy, she would be gone.

Kristin strutted through the foyer of the gym, heading directly to the woman's locker room.

There were a dozen women in the room, most wrapped in towels, others getting into their gym attire. A few nodded her direction, but for the most part they ignored her. Kristin found a corner where she was not observed, put down the gym bag, removed the jacket and quickly put on what she had brought with her. She stuffed the jacket in the gym bag and headed for the back door.

She exited the rear of the gym into the alleyway, her disguise complete. It has taken less than one minute for the change, and now her shoulder length blond hair was hidden up under the hat she had brought, and the pedestrian looking skirt and blouse, along with the flat undistinguishable shoes completed the transformation from debutant to average Washington, DC working woman. She made the street and looked back. Both agents were still talking, right there in front of the building. That made Kristin smile.

The first meeting was about five blocks away. The Starbucks was less than two blocks from the White House, and even closer to a series of offices used by the various federal departments needing overflow space. She saw the middle-aged man, sitting exactly where she had directed him to be. Kristin slid into the chair directly opposite him, depositing the gym bag on the third vacant chair. Kristin wasted no time, pulling the document still in its envelope from her handbag and handed it to the man, who accepted it hesitantly.

"Once this is done, I owe you nothing more," the man stated. His voice low, lest anyone overhear them.

"That's correct," Kristin stated.

The man nodded, standing, hesitated and turned back to her.

"If they discover that I did this, there will be trouble," he stated flatly.

"That's when having friends in high places, will be even more valuable, but they won't discover that you had anything to do with it. I've already insured that it will appear that the document was misplaced within the maze of systems your office maintains. You have nothing to worry about, and you will have a friend in a very high place indeed," Kristin said.

The man's eyes flashed a worried and at the same time angry glare at her. The word friend she had stated in a most seductive tone, calling to mind his transgression, that event, which had put him in her debt. That falling seemed to be forever before him costing him more than he ever imagined the experience would.

He turned to move away.

"Say hi to your wife for me, Jean hasn't been at the gym lately, I hope everything is okay?" Kristin said.

The man did not stop or turn towards her. Kristin knew this final reminder of her proximity to his wife would seal his resolve. A misplaced, misspoken word by Kristin, and his marriage would detonate and dissolve in flames. Kristin suspected that she would never see Jean again, they would move to another community, or something would arise to prevent Jean from being in the same circle of friends, but, her one-night romance with Jacob Weinstein, had done the trick. She had someone in the bureaucracy perfectly placed for what she needed done.

She had heard his name mentioned as a potential for the Treasury Secretary position in the new cabinet. Kristin knew he would never accept the position, not with Jim Rosewood as the Vice President. That would be to close for comfort for Jacob. Kristin smiled to herself. If he did take the position, that would be just fine. His dalliance was a gift that kept giving for Kristin.

The phone vibrated in her bag, getting her attention.

It was Avery. His voice upset.

"I'm here, where are you?" his statement and question short and clipped.

"You're early, and I am on my way," Kristin responded, closing the phone, preventing any further communication. She glanced at the time on the phone and noted that she was in fact, on time.

Kristin walked the three blocks at a leisurely pace, arriving at the Grill exactly at 8:00 AM, the time she had told Avery she would be there. The Brick Street Grill was one of those restaurants set up for meetings, each table neatly walled off from those surrounding it, allowing even more privacy than most restaurants. Kristin knew that many of the political insiders favored this Grill exactly for its privacy. Many deals were cut over a drink, a meal, and a cigar. This grill, somehow, had escaped the smoking ban, and cigars were still allowed, and even sold like food at the grill.

A wall full of pictures showing the powerful and famous who had visited the grill greeted you when you walked in the door, secrecy without anonymity. The place reeked of deal making. There was even a picture of Jim Rosewood and several other senators that had met here in the past. This was one of the few times, Kristin was pleased to note, that there was no picture of her. She did stop for a moment and consider the picture of her husband. In the background there was a woman, seemingly passing by as the picture was taken, but there was something familiar about her. Kristin had little time to consider this, as she saw Avery Moment, sitting in the booth with the least amount of shielding. It was just like Avery, he never had the sophistication his brother had.

Kristin walked quickly to the booth and slid all the way in, on the opposite side from Avery. This had the desired effect, forcing Avery to also slide away from the opening, and at least partially giving them both some anonymity.

Avery Moment was still a handsome man, but where his brother had been thin and tall with a creamy white complexion and a regal mob of premature graying hair, Avery was short, muscular, with an olive skin color that spoke of middle eastern or Latin decent and a full head of dark hair. Kristin noted that he had also added a closely clipped beard to his appearance. It was, as if, he was trying to prove he was still a man. This made Kristin smile again. Where Hastings had been confident and self- assured, Avery was reserved, and if anything, even a little shy. Kristin had never discovered the genesis of either Hastings or Avery Moment, and other than their claim to being brothers, there was nothing in their appearance that would have provided evidence of that kinship.

"You're late," Avery asserted again.

Kristin glanced at her watch. It was 8:02 AM. She chose to ignore his statement.

A waiter that Kristin recognized arrived before Kristin could answer. She ordered coffee and her usual, a bowl of fruit and yogurt. Avery order the largest breakfast steak and omelet on the menu. Kristin had to smile, Avery was in every way trying to prove he was still a man. She knew he would never have ordered that breakfast if he had been alone. He saw her smile, and she could see he had read it correctly, his face contorting into a sneer, and the manic light of insanity flickering in his eyes. The waiter left, and before Avery could say anything else, Kristin said, "Okay, Avery, what is it going to cost me?"

"Cost you?" Avery's tone confused.

"Yes, you said that I had promised you something, that I am not going to give you, so in the end I need to know what is it going to cost me?" Kristin summed up the whole reason for the meeting and the ground rules for the outcome.

She knew that Avery had to know there was no way she was giving him what he had asked for, especially when she was this close to achieving her own desires. She watched as the emotions rippled through Avery's face. She saw in his eyes the blaze that indicated that he was close to losing whatever control he may still exercise over his emotions. Avery was definitely unbalanced, and her comment had come close to unhinging whatever last hold he had on sanity. The storm passed, and the blaze in his eyes simmered to a smoldering cloud.

"I want what is mine. I paid you for keeping her, and I am her father. I want her to know me" Avery said.

Kristin had no doubt what type of knowing Avery had in mind.

Kristin considered Avery again. Her next words would either push him over the edge to insanity or pull him back and perhaps restore a little reason to his demented mind.

"Listen Avery, I know she is likely the only evidence you have that you were ever a man" those words rekindling the blaze in his eyes.

She moved on quickly.

"But I also think you know, that she is now under the protection of the Secret Service, and that the amount of attention her disappearance would cause is more than either you, or I can afford. In some ways, if you took her, it might be better for me, the grieving mother, the wife of the next Vice President of the US, sharing with the world how much her daughter means to her.

They would catch you I am sure, and then what? Do you think they would believe for a moment your story, if they take you alive? Sure, they might be able to prove you are her father, but it would be after you had a bullet in your head, and you would not be around to gloat over your victory. So, what you want makes no sense, for either of us. So again, what is it going to cost me, to get you out of my life forever?" Kristin said.

The light of sanity seemed to disappear and reappear in the man's eyes. She could almost hear the conversation that was raging within his mind. Finally, he looked at her and said, "Two Hundred and Fifty Million."

Kristin knew that was the number that most of the media had stated as her net worth. He wanted to strip her of all her supposed monetary wealth. She let the shocked look sweep across her face, allowing her head to shake as if what he had asked was too much.

"Two Hundred and Fifty Million," he stated again, his eyes now shining with triumph.

Kristin realized that he needed to humiliate her in some way, to come away from this meeting thinking of himself as the victor. She let her eyes drop, as if she was thinking through the implications of her giving up all her supposed wealth. Finally, she let her eyes met his again.

"If I give you what you are asking for, I need some guarantee that you will in fact keep your side of the bargain," Kristin said.

"I'm not the one who broke the bargain" Avery shot back.

"My word is good, I've never not done what I said I was going to do," he added.

She just looked at him, allowing him to again see doubt, as if that was really racing through her mind. She shook her head again, as if she had decided against the request.

"I'll promise to leave the country and never return," Avery added, his eyes communicating what his thoughts were, he was thinking that his only possible victory was sliding away.

Kristin stopped again, looking at him. A full minute passed. Kristin watched his eyes, seeing Avery dancing between gloating in triumph and then plunging into anger just shy of pure insanity. She reached down to her pocket book and removed a small pad of paper and wrote something on it. She tore the piece of paper out of the book and slid it across the table to him.

"You call me when you are at Kennedy airport and on the plane. I'll transfer the money to this account at this bank, when I have verified that you have left these shores, and Avery, I am going to get your name put on the list that will alert me, if you ever return to this country. If you do, so help me I will find a way to silence you forever," Kristin said.

Kristin saw the gleam of fading sanity, and then saw it flicker back on.

"I'll be on a plane tomorrow, you can check, I bought the ticket last week. I'm not telling you where I am ending up, but I'll be out of your life," Avery said.

Apparently, he had been sane enough to already have thought this through. He obviously had done the research into how much she was worth, and unlike his brother, had assumed that what was published was accurate. He also had not put up half the struggle she would have, if getting Susan had ever really been his end game. It had always been the money.

Kristin congratulated herself for the conclusion she had come to. It had surprised her when Avery wrote that he still wanted Susan, four years after the original proposed date. A little research and she had discovered that Avery Moment was close to bankruptcy. Without his brother, he had lost the considerable fortune he had made with his brother. She stood picking up the gym bag and her handbag.

"Just send me a message when you are on the plane. You can check for the funds from the plane as well, and you will see that they are there. Have a nice life Avery with all of your money, and stay out of mine," Kristin said.

Kristin rose from the table, even as the waiter returned.

"He's paying, and he can eat mine as well," Kristin said, smiling at Avery.

The final comment meant to drive doubt into Avery's mind. Her voice had not communicated defeat, but defiance and confidence. He thought he had come out on top, but Kristin wanted him to know, she had gotten exactly what she had come for.

Kristin left the restaurant, not looking back to see what Avery did. She glanced at her watch, 8:43 AM stared back at her. She had less than ten minutes to make it back to the gym. It started raining on her way back. She made it, with two minutes to spare, but when she got to the alley, she glanced down it, and saw the agent standing by the door, but looking the wrong way. She quickly returned to the street. They must have discovered she was not in the gym.

She walked quickly to another alley, and turned into it, seeing the large metal trash container tucked beside the back door to the store. No one was in the alley. She walked to the dumpster, removed her blouse, skirt and shoes and threw them into the open container getting soaked to the skin with only the body stocking covering her.

Opening her gym bag, she quickly put back on her shoes, and slipped her coat over her body stocking. She returned to the street and headed back to the front of the gym. Her limo was still there, and there were four other agents standing talking, with her driver in the middle of them. They all appeared oblivious to the rain. They did not see her approach. When she got to the limo, she said in a loud voice.

"Earl, are you going to leave me standing here in the rain?"

That got all of their attention. When they turned, the saw her, in the same outfit she had worn into the gym, with the same gym bag, waiting.

Earl quickly returned and opened the door for her.

The senior agent, the one with the perpetual frown, stuck his head in the door before Earl could close it.

"Mrs. Rosewood, where have you been?" he said.

"What you mean, where have I been, I've been in the gym exercising, that is where I have been!" Kristin said as indignantly as she could.

"We checked, and you were not there. Where have you been?" the agent asked again.

"Did you check the sauna room, I don't think any of the ladies would have been happy if you guys just waltzed in on us, but then, none of you did, so you didn't find me either," Kristin said.

"Earl, take me home, I have a lot going on today, and I am not letting these bozo's mess up my schedule," she demanded.

The senior agent's eyes had flickered, a moment of doubt passing through them. Kristin relished the moment. He did not know whether his agents had checked the sauna. Kristin reached out, grabbed the door handle and pulled the door closed, almost catching the agent as he moved his head and hand at the last moment. Would have served him right, if she had clunked his head, or hand, or both, she thought. Such incompetence, they had lost track of her, and they thought she would explain what had happened. Not likely.

She punched the close widow button and watched as her compartment was once again sealed off from Earl and his roving eyes as well. She allowed herself to relax for the first time all morning. She had done it. She had handled two of her problems and now she was free to focus on the rest of the day.

When she arrived at her residence the senior agent was already there. He followed her through the foyer and into the elevator, with two of the other agents in tow. He said nothing, until she was at her front door. Kristin unlocked the door, and was opening it when he said,

"Mrs. Rosewood, mam, I must apologize for what just happened. It turns out, we had not checked the sauna. If you would tell me a few of the names of the ladies there with you, we will be happy to put this incident behind us," he said, not sounding all that apologetic. He obviously did not believe her story.

Kristin just stared back at him.

She unzipped her jacket removing it, turned to the front door, entered her residence and let the door slam in the agent's face. Kristin saw the impact of her action on the two younger agents, and for the first time, she saw surprise, and something else register on the senior agents' face. Perhaps he was human after all, she thought.

Chapter 7 – Understanding

Ken looked at Jenny Housher. The woman had obviously been shaken by something, but she had said nothing other than, "John, Chi, I need to go home."

"I'll take you home Jenny," Ken volunteered.

"Thanks Ken," his father said, seconding his thoughts.

It was obvious to Ken, that Jenny was in no emotional condition to drive, even the three short blocks to her house, just a block away from the school where her husband had taught.

"I doubt we will need your further Mrs. Housher, but if we do, we will let you know. Thanks for all of your help so far," Agent Smithers said as Jenny headed for the door.

Ken noticed that she had been unable to look at either Jim or Susan House as she walked to the door. Obviously, her upset was in some way connected to the arrival of Buddy's two children, but he could not figure out how they would have upset her.

Jim House was an exceptional student, and his reputation in the small town was exemplarity. If it had been possible, his presence in the town had replaced much of the shame attached to the House name. Both he, and his sister Susan, had been living with their grandparents, Kristin's parents, for the last six years, and they were accepted Hitchenburgh residents. Even Susan, was well respected in the small town, and she had made quite a name for herself, both as a student and as a female athlete.

She was the high school leading scorer in basketball, and she had led the school's volley ball team to the county championship. On top of that, she also was drop dead gorgeous, and was following in her brothers' footsteps, heading to college at the same Christian school, he was graduating from this year as well. She was the class valedictorian for the high school, and Ken had just learned that Jim House was the class valedictorian for the college graduating class as well. All told, an amazing tribute to both young people who had such unusually dysfunctional parents.

Ken walked with Jenny to her car, opening the door for her. She had handed him the keys to the car, making no protest about her ability to drive herself home. She had said nothing, until Ken had pulled in front of her house.

"Ken, would you come inside, I need to show you something," she said.

Ken followed her dutifully to the door. Once inside the house, Ken had stood in the living room, while Jenny had gone upstairs. She returned moments later, her coat off, carrying a picture frame in her hands.

'Sit down Ken, please," Jenny said.

Ken sat, and Jenny took a seat across from him.

"Do you know the story of what happened to my husband Craig?" Julie asked.

Ken nodded.

"Buddy blackmailed him, wanted money from him, and he committed suicide" Ken said. Watching Julie carefully to make sure the reliving of that history would not send her over another emotional cliff.

"Do you know what Buddy was blackmailing him with?" she asked.

"No," Ken admitted. There was nothing in the files at the station about what had led to Craig's suicide. Ken had looked, and all that was there were the notes indicating that he had been distraught over the demands and had shot himself.

Jenny told Ken the story that was missing from the records.

At the end, she said, "Craig admitted to me that he had slept with Kristin. It was during the trip to MIT when he had taken her, his star pupil, to meet the folks there. He had told me, he was sure that Kristin Bloaden was going to be someone famous. Of course, he was thinking she was going to make a name for herself in science. Did you know she has a 186 IQ? She was the most brilliant person Craig had ever met. She was brilliant and gorgeous.

She also apparently has no scruples at all, about taking what was not hers. Buddy was using her relationships with several the teachers." She saw the question in Ken's eyes and answered it before he could ask. "Yes, there were more than just Craig. Buddy used that knowledge to get the money to start his business ventures. He married her, despite her obvious lack of any morals to speak of. You could say that Kristin and Buddy were made for one another. All though Buddy seems to have changed." Jenny's voice falling an octave at the last comment.

Ken listened to the story, piecing together many parts of other stories based on what he was hearing.

"But what upset you, Jenny? Did the presence of Buddy and his children, bring back these memories?", Ken asked.

Jenny said nothing. Standing she walked over and handed Ken the picture.

Ken looked at the picture. It was a much younger Jenny, the resemblance to the now seventy-year-old woman in front of him still crystal clear. She was holding a young boy, already a chunky toddler, which must be her son John, and she was standing beside a man. Ken did a double take, the man was just slightly taller than Jenny, but was handsome. The black and white picture did not reveal the color of his hair, but it was swept back, and his face had a broad smile on it. Ken looked at the picture and then back at Jenny. He understood now, what had upset her at his father's home.

"I don't think Buddy knows," Jenny said.

"I didn't realize it, until today, when he came in with his sister. I couldn't tell Buddy, with everything he has been through, this might truly kill him," Jenny said.

"I knew there was something else bothering Craig. He confessed freely his sin, asking me to forgive him. I was so shocked, I could not fathom his breaking his vows with any woman, and especially not a student. He was a Christian, taught bible studies right in this house. His favorite story was of David and Bathsheba. He knew that story inside out, yet he fell just like David did. But unlike David, he was so ashamed, he took his own life, and now I know why. Until today, it never made sense to me, but now I know what probably pushed him over the edge. He knew," Jenny concluded.

Ken just nodded.

"Buddy's got to be told, but I can't do it Ken. And that poor boy, what is Jim going to think when he realizes not only that Buddy is not his father, but just what type of woman his mother is." Jenny added.

"Can I take the picture, Jenny?" Ken asked.

She nodded. Ken stood heading for the door.

"Jenny, I am so sorry," Ken said as he passed through the opening. "I'm sure that Craig loved you and John very much," Ken said, trying to salvage something for Jenny Houser.

Tears leaked out of Jenny's eyes.

"Yes, he loved us both very much, just not enough," Jenny said, as the door closed.

Ken walked back the three blocks towards his father's house. He used the time to think through how he was going to broach what he had just learned.

Ken did not ring the doorbell this time, as the door was cracked open, as if expecting his rapid return. He walked in and saw that the two agents had left. Buddy was talking with Jim and Susan. Ken motioned to Glenn and to his father. Both John and Chi were listening to the conversation as well, and stayed seated despite being aware of Ken's presence.

Glenn and Ken's father stood and moved towards Ken. Buddy and the two young people did not seem to notice, lost in conversation. Together the three men slid into the kitchen area.

"Jenny all right?" Ken's father asked.

"Not really," he said, handing his father the picture frame, without comment. Ken saw the color drain out of his father's face, and he handed the picture over to Glenn. Unlike his father, Glenn either did not make the connection or wasn't surprised by what the picture revealed.

"Explains a lot," Glenn said, revealing it was the latter.

"We have to tell Buddy and Jim, it's going to come out sooner or later. But how do we do it?," Ken said.

"How do you do what," the young man's voice broke in.

All three men turned to see Jim House standing watching them. How much he had heard, Ken did not know. They had not seen him stand or heard his approach. Jim walked towards Glenn. It was obvious that he understood that the picture Glenn was holding had something to do with him. Glenn handed him the picture.

Jim appraised the picture, his eyes registering the surprise as he connected the import of what it revealed.

"The man, that's John's father, Jenny's husband?," Jim asked more as confirmation.

"Yes, it is," Glenn said.

"What's going on Jim?," Susan's voice causing the four men now to turn. Behind her was Buddy, and behind Buddy stood John and Chi.

"Let's go back to the living room," Glenn suggested.

Three hours later, they all departed Ken's father's home, except for Buddy, who was staying with Pastor Farr until the agents came back to pick him up. Buddy thought that would be by Friday, but it all depended on how successful they were with conducting the arrests they already had clearance to do. For the first time in many years, Buddy was not under close supervision. But Buddy had changed, he wasn't running anymore.

"Pastor, if it is all right with you, I'll just head up to my old room?" Buddy had said.

Ken's father nodded, knowing that Buddy and Glenn both knew the house as well as he did. Jim and Susan were headed over to John's mother's home with John and Chi. Amazingly, Jim and Buddy both took the discovery well. It was Susan that had caused the greatest concern when she had asked:

"If Buddy is not Jim's real father, then who is my real father?"

Ken realized, that Susan had figured out sometime ago, that Buddy wasn't her biological father.

Amazingly, it was Buddy who answered her question. Just when Buddy had made the connection, Ken did not know, but it was obvious that he had asked the same question well before the discoveries of this day.

It took more than an hour of talking before Susan finally seemed to accept the situation. The whole time Chi had sat next to her, and when Susan finally broke down, she had held Susan as if she were her own daughter.

Buddy looked worn out. He had finally concluded saying, "Jim and Susan, you never asked to have the parents you have. On my part I was too enthralled with my own plans to even wonder about what is now so obvious. But, when I look back now, the best that came out of your mom, is the two of you. I know you deserve better, heaven knows I deserve a lot worse, but I want to be a part of your lives now. For better or worse, I always believed you where my children, and I cannot replace your real fathers, but I want to try and fill the gap I helped create."

Both of the young adults seemed to accept Buddy's words as genuine. Both had hugged him before they had left with John and Chi. John had also surprised everyone.

"It may take mom a while to get use to the idea, but I think mom is going to like the fact that I have a brother. And Susan, mom always talked about the fact that my dad and her had dreamed of having a daughter. You are Jim's sister, and that makes you family as well," he added.

The house had emptied quickly, the consensus was that everyone would get together again tomorrow, to wait and watch for the unfolding of the actions that were underway. Ken looked at his watch. It was approaching Five PM. Buddy had gone upstairs, leaving just Glenn, Ken's father and Ken downstairs in the kitchen.

"I've got to go to the office Dad. Can you do dinner with me in a couple of hours?" Ken asked.

Ken felt them, before Ken's father had a chance to answer. He turned to see the two figures seemingly materializing just inside the front door. Whether they had walked through the closed door, or just popped in from somewhere else, Ken did not know. They were unchanged. The one figure shrouded with a deep majestic blue while the smaller figure gleamed with a turquoise color. Ken saw his father smile and heard his greeting to the two figures.

It was another hour before Ken left to return to the sheriff's office. Glenn walked out with the two angels, the familiar "clack, clack, clack" of his staff marking his steps. Ken went to the door expecting to see the three figures descending the steps, but they were gone.

Ken made it home by eleven-thirty but did not make it to bed until well after two AM. He had looked in on his children, both sound asleep, and had planted kisses on both children's foreheads. Ken spent the next two hours explaining to Bernice all that had happened and preparing her for the storm he knew was coming.

Chapter 8 – The Center of Attention

Kristin basked in the memory of the day. It was the second-best day of her life, she decided, topped only by one other. The reception for the visiting Russian president was the coming out party that had been marred by the annoying question of the reporter less than twenty-four hours ago. For Kristin, the reception confirmed her belief that she belonged in the center of the power that emanated from the people there. She had fit right in. The drive back to the residence gave her time to relive the event.

After the successful morning adventure handling both her problems with Avery Moment and the pesky and persistent IRS, Kristin had escaped to the luxury of an hour-long soak in her tub. She discovered that Jim was gone for the day, finding his note on the credenza, at the same spot where the earlier mail had sent her on her morning mission.

"Kristin, off to New York for the first round of interviews with three of the networks.

Should be back in time for the reception at the White House for the Russian President. I'll see you there. Don't be late, as I will get there right at 6:30 PM. Wear something conservative. I don't think we should be the center of attention yet. Later, Jim." It was so like Jim, thinking he could control her. Kristin smiled to herself.

"Conservative", she had exactly the outfit to fit that bill. She had bought it for herself during their last visit to France. The black evening gown fit like a glove, but lacked either the plunging neck line, or the hip level slits that Kristin preferred. Yes, it was more conservative, except for the nearly half million dollars' worth of diamonds laced into the outfit, outline every curve with sparkling effect. Jim had loved it, telling her it was even more provocative than so many of her more daring outfits. This one turned heads as well. Kristin was sure it would provide exactly the effect she desired.

With terry cloth bathrobe covering her she headed to the office immediately after her bath. Sitting at her computer she brought up the one file. The blinking cursor indicating a new recording.

She smiled to herself as she watched the performance of her and Jim from the previous night.

She deleted the file. Nothing to be gained from keeping it. Each room in the suite was wired similarly, and all of the bedrooms and bathrooms had provided plenty of valuable footage.

Kristin regularly updated the secure storage with new additions.

Between her Blackberry and her video files, she could compete with anything any of the numerous madam's in DC could expose. Her first husband had the right idea, for whatever reason nothing bought faster allegiance or compliance than the threat of exposure of sexual dalliances. For Kristin, that was almost humorous. How was it that people were so fearful of something that brought so much pleasure? Surely if it felt good, it was good. But she accepted and readily used other people's fears to her own benefit.

She glanced at the clock. It was only a little before noon. The maid would be here soon.

Kristin walked back to the master bedroom. It was still a mess, the evening activities visually displayed to the trained eye. Kristin retired to one of the spare bedrooms. She would prefer catching a nap in a clean bed. The maid knew that if the spare bedroom door was closed, she needn't check it. There was plenty of time for her nap.

Kristin woke a little before three. The suite was still silent. She grabbed a quick snack from the kitchen and had just finished when the phone rang. It was Jim's executive assistant. A clipped English accent matched the dour image that immediately flashed before Kristin's eyes when she heard the voice.

"Mrs. Rosewood, it's Jan," the voice said.

"Yes. What's up?" Kristin responded, mirroring the clipped nasally tone.

"Senator Rosewood is delayed in New York, he might not make it back in time for the reception. He wants you to attend the reception anyway, and the President has made preparations for an escort for this evening's event. General Tony McIntyre will be your escort for the evening. The Senator said he should see you later this evening, probably back at the residence," and then she had hung up, waiting for no response.

Kristin fumed at the audacity of the woman. But she had found Jan for Jim, and she was perfect. There was nothing about the woman to cause any problems with Jim. She was a dumpy fifty-year-old, who was bright and efficient, and completely without any interest in anything other than the money the position provided.

General Tony McIntyre, newly widower, and the current Chairman of the Joint Chiefs was her escort. "How interesting," Kristin thought.

Being the VP's wife was going to be a lot of fun. The reception wasn't to start until 7:00 PM. Plenty of time to get ready. By 6:00 PM she was ready.

The last little touches of makeup and she examined her image. She was perfect.

The secret service agents, who had seen her more revealing costume in the morning, did a real double take when she emerged from her suite for the drive to the White House. She enjoyed the awareness that neither agent could take their eyes off her, all the way to where Earl was parked waiting for her. She loved every moment of it.

She arrived at the entrance to the White House, and saw the tall 6' 6" general with his trade mark bald head, waiting for her. Kristin strolled leisurely from her limousine to the general. She noticed his appreciative stare as he took in her dazzling outfit.

"Mrs. Rosewood, it's a pleasure to meet you," the General's voice a mixture of Midwestern accent and amusement.

"The president told me, you were a beautiful woman, and I have seen you on the television before, but neither his description or the TV do the real you justice," the general concluded.

The man's reputation for frank speech was well earned Kristin noted. Most men would had kept their impressions of her to themselves. She smiled at the General.

"You are very kind General. And thank you for filling in for Jim, I am sure you had another suitable date for the reception, and I appreciate you changing your plans," Kristin said, shaking the general's offered hand and reaching up planting a kiss firmly on his check.

"When the president calls, you typically change your plans," the general answered, a laugh bracketing the comment, and a flush coloring his face.

`Together Kristin and the general joined the line, entering the reception. For the next half hour Kristin had followed the General's lead, each new couple or individual name being recorded in Kristin's mind. It was a who's who, of the Washington elite. Even two supreme court justices and the Chief Justice were there as well as the Majority and Minority leaders of the Senate, and the Speaker of the House. At least another fifty senators and representatives with their wives or dates also milled around waiting in little clumps like disorganized cells waiting for something to bring them all together. All told, there must have been close to four hundred people in various conversations, waiting.

At about seven o'clock the president was announced along with the new Russian president. Kristin noted that the current vice president and his wife were nowhere to be seen. It was as if he had already been replaced by the newly announced Vice-Presidential candidate. Of course Jim was not here either which left Kristin to take up the slack.

After the announcement, the president had made a bee line towards Kristin and the General, with the Russian President, the wives of each president, and several others in tow. Just before reaching them, Kristin watched as the president's wife had stopped, causing the Russian presidents' wife to stop as well, to greet several attendees that had been passed by the President.

"Mr. President, this is General Tony McIntyre," the president said. Making the first introduction.

Kristin listened as one of the men bracketing the Russian President, translated the comments into Russian for him. Kristin noted that the translator had added General McIntyre's role to the title. She also noted that the Russian president had not taken his eyes off her since they were ten feet away from the general and herself.

"And this is Kristin Rosewood, the Vice President's wife. Jim could not be here this evening, but I am pleased to say that Kristin was able to join us for the reception. He's up in New York making the necessary media rounds, based on his upcoming new role." The president said. The error by the president not even raising the eyebrows of those that would know the error.

Kristin listened as the translator who had also seen the two women stopping some thirty feet away, and who understood the delay of those women reaching this meeting. They were surrounded by the other visitors wanting to meet both the First Lady and the Russian President's wife and the provided an opportunity for additional frankness, since no one would understand the conversation between the translator and the Russian president.

In his translation had added several not so subtle additions for the president's behalf.

"Mr. President, this is the woman you wanted to meet. This is Kristin Rosewood, the Vice President's wife. Her husband is in New York being interviewed. You were right, she is quite the looker," he had said to the president.

It was obvious that they knew that neither the president or the general knew Russian.

She was sure that whatever dossier they had on her, did not show her fluency.

"Her husband must be one lucky fellow. I doubt I would let her out of the bedroom if I was him," the Russian president quipped to his translator.

"The president says, he is glad to make your acquaintance Mrs. Rosewood."

"I appreciate the opportunity as well, and am especially flattered that you believe my husband is fortunate. He seems to enjoy our bedroom just fine," Kristin said in faultless Russian, accenting the 'fine' in such a way as to leave no doubt as to what was being inferred.

That got their attention, and the Russian President turned several shades of red deeper than his already dark complexion.

"I told the president, I was glad to make his acquaintance as well, "Kristin said to the US president, who was looking just as shocked as the Russian president, but not from understanding.

"You speak Russian?" the US president asked.

"Yes, a hangover from my school days, when most of the math and science of interest was in Russian" Kristin said.

Kristin heard the Russian translator accurately communicate both the question and Kristin's answer.

The two presidents' wives joined the group, having made the transition finally to their husband's sides. Maggie, the US president's wife, was a trim and proper woman of fifty, with short cut dark hair surrounding a pleasant face with sparkling brown eyes. Kristin knew her reputation as a sharp and politically savvy spouse, who had both guided and supported her husband through much of his political career. Behind every successful man there was a strong woman., Kristin thought, and the president's wife was a proof in point.

They had two children, both mirror images of their parents. Kristin had met Maggie several times over the years in DC. She had never been very cordial to Kristin, always acting as if Kristin was something beneath her. Even Kristin's substantial contribution to her husbands' current presidential campaign had not warmed her up. The woman eyed Kristin, with the look of suspicion that only one woman could read from another. It was clear, they were not going to be friends. She nodded at Kristin and turned to her husband.

"Henry, the new Chinese ambassador is here as well. Perhaps the President would like to make her acquaintance as well, "Maggie said, distracting her husband from his contemplations on Kristin's revelation and her provocative dress.

Again, the Russian translator had translated flawlessly the statement.

The president had nodded and turned to follow his wife. The Russian president and the general turned to follow them. Kristin walked beside the general, and she noted how many stopped and watched the small group pass. She knew there was plenty of interest in the two presidents, but she also could tell that they were only part of the draw, she saw it in the eyes of both the men and the women. There was no doubt her dress was turning heads. They would be talking about her, long after the reception was done. That's what she wanted. The focus of attention was on her. She recognized envy and lust when she saw it, but in this case the cause was both the desire to be in the group surrounding the two presidents, and a more blatant wishing from the women to be like her, and from the men to be closer to her. She was in her element.

Soon, they were all standing surrounding a small petite woman, the first Chinese woman ever to hold an ambassadorship, and certainly one of the few female ambassadors to the US from any country. Again, all the perfunctory introductions, followed by a series of pleasantries which were normal at these functions. The Chinese ambassador had four attendants, two of which appeared to take turns translating the comments for the Chinese ambassador. Finally, she had raised her hand, quieting their translation.

"Mr, Presidents, I appreciate the opportunity to meet both of you at the same time. I am sure, that our time together will be profitable for all of our countries," she had said first in English, and then in passable Russian. Neither president seemed surprised by her fluency, and Kristin was sure that they had both been briefed on her fluency.

The woman had acknowledged Kristin, but had said little to her during the next ten minutes of banter that had continued. It was only as the group was breaking up that she had turned to Kristin , smiled and said, in Chinese, "You must be especially proud of your husband, reaching such great heights, in such a short time."

Kristin had responded in flawless Chinese, "I am. Of course you already knew that I understood Chinese, you just wanted to be sure, correct?," The ambassador smiled, patted her hand, and slid away into the circle of senators approaching her for the next round of questions.

"She is a very smart woman," the Russian translator said.

Kristin turned eyeing the man who had made the error earlier of assuming that she wasn't fluent in Russian.

"You understood her question," Kristin asked.

"No, but I understood that she got what she wanted, she knows that you also understand Chinese, she's not about to make the same mistake I did. By the way, you said that you learned Russian for your studies of math and science, may I ask what papers were so important for you to learn our language?", he asked.

Kristin eyed the man, wondering what his game was. After a minute of thinking she could see no harm, so she told him. He listened and then surprised her with his next comment.

"I read a paper by a US mathematician, I was a young person then, in Russia studying at the institute similar to your MIT here, I had the opportunity to read her paper. I later learned it had been written by a high school student, not even a college student yet. The paper showed a remarkable understanding of some very complex issues involved in wave theory. That paper drew me into wanting to understand English better. Math is a universal language, but the explanation of the intention and reasoning behind the math isn't. So, you see, you and I have very similar experiences Mrs. Rosewood."

Kristin's heart seemed to be beating louder, she could hear it in her own ears, thundering.

"Do you remember the name of the paper?" Kristin asked.

He told her.

Kristin saw the General approaching. She had smiled again at the translator, and said, "Life has many strange experiences, it is not surprising that we were both drawn to our current positions by similar ones."

Kristin turned and walked towards the general, while her mind whirled lost in pleasure.

He had read her paper. He had not realized it had been her paper, it came from a different life time. But her paper had made it all the way to Russia, and to a school there where her work was apparently shown as something unique. Jim Housher had been her teacher, her only one true love and he had been right. Someday she would be someone important. She wondered, what he would think of her now. She shook that thought away. She would not go down that memory road again.

The rest of the evening had continued just getting better. She had been accepted into the various conversations going on, and before long many of the people were listening to her ideas, and comments. She was going to be a force to be reckoned with, and that thought was better than any drug.

Kristin arrived back at the residence, and once again the Secret Service agents trailed her all the way to her door. Once inside Kristin made it to the kitchen, reaching for a glass and the bottle of her favorite wine.

"Have a nice night, "the slurred voice of her husband said.

Kristin turned, startled, both by his presence and by his obviously inebriated condition.

He looked terrible. He held a large tumbler in one hand and a half empty Jim Bean whiskey bottle in the other. His tie was missing, but he had not taken off his suit jacket. He looked rumpled from top to bottom.

"What happened to you?" Kristin asked, truly disturbed both by his appearance and his demeanor. This was so unlike Jim. She had seen him drunk before, but he was typically jovial and playful when in that condition. He was neither tonight. He just stared at her.

"What happened to me?" he repeated.

"You did," he finally answered. And then turned and walked to the master bedroom, slamming the door solidly behind him. Kristin stared at the door, and made the decision to sleep in the spare bedroom. It would do no good to try and ply out of him what had happened to turn him so morbid. Besides, once he was sober, her news from the evening should help ease whatever concerns had driven him to the bottle.

As Kristin slid under the covers of the bed in the spare bedroom, she was still mulling over Jim's strange comment and basking in the memories of the evening. It took a while for her to fall asleep.

She slipped into the dream or was it the memory?

She was walking hand in hand with her former teacher and lover. It was truly a wonderful dream, they had a child, and together they were happy, they were a family, she really had what she desired most. She was his center of attention. The house was old, but neat, he was looking out of the window. She was so happy. He was hers. She ran to him and threw her arms around him. He turned to her smiling, telling her she was beautiful and bright.

"Just what am I going to do with you," his words causing her insides to melt all over again. They kissed, the kisses passionate and full of energy. He had been right, her paper was just the beginning. Together they would be something truly important. They were in bed, making love, making their son, it was the most wonderful night of her life. The dream changed.

She saw the woman approaching her lover, she hit him with something heavy, and he fell on the floor. Then the gun appeared, she placed it in his mouth, and pulled the trigger. Her jerked once and was still.

"No, No! " she heard herself crying out. Anger and sadness sweeping over her as she ran towards the woman, to stop her, to undo what she had done. She got to the woman and whipped her around, ready to strike her with all the strength she could muster. Her hand was raised, ready to strike. But the woman just smiled at her.

Kristin woke with a start. It was still dark, she looked over at the clock, it said it was 3:30 AM. She remembered the dream clearly, it was just a nightmare. She got up went to the bathroom and turned on the light.

Staring back at her from the mirror was a woman. She gasped, it was the woman that had been smiling at her in the dream.

Chapter 9 – A Puzzle

Ken stood beneath the tree again, staring up. He knew he had been missing something important here. Even with only a few hours of sleep, he awoke thinking about Hasting Moments unsolved murder. That murder held a key, to unlock so many of the mysteries that seemed to swirl around him. He knew that the angels were not omnipotent or omnipresent, but he felt that they knew something they were not sharing, at least not with him. He had questioned Glenn about what he knew, and it was obvious that Glenn knew even less than he did. It was strange that someone so often in the company of these heavenly beings was even more in the dark about what had happened to Hastings than he was.

Ken had spent time with his father as well. Preparing for the announcement of the courts' decision, talking over the strange circumstances that had brought a supposedly dead Buddy House back into their lives, and wondering about the discovery of the parentage for both Jim House and Susan House, took up much of the time. All those issues were more than enough to keep Ken and Ken's father busy, but Ken could not help but continue peppering his father with questions related to the case. Ken found his father's answers even less helpful than normal. When his father had said, "Why don't we pray on it for a while," Ken's frustrations had boiled over.

"Dad, I need answers, there is something I'm missing, I know it, and I can't find out what it is. If the angels don't know, or won't help, and Glenn knows even less than I do, what makes you think that praying is going to help?"

Ken remembered his father's patient stare, and Ken realized the answer to his own question. He wasn't praying to creatures, but to someone who was both omnipotent and omnipresent. Finally, he broke down and joined his father in prayer. But by the time he left his father's house to return home, he still had no answers. Once again, he was convinced that the time praying had been wasted.

He looked over at Bernice, her peaceful face, still at rest. She was truly beautiful even as she lie there sleeping. He closed his eyes again, wishing for a few more minutes of sleep.

"God, why won't you tell me what I am missing? Why do you let my mind keep coming back to his death if you aren't going to show me what I am missing?" Ken's prayer both a petition and a complaint.

Ken opened his eyes again, took in his wife's still sleeping form, and froze. The thought almost audible in his ears, he looked around, thinking for sure, it had been a voice. The luminous dials of the alarm clock and the slowly creeping dawn provided light enough for Ken to know, it was just the two of them in the bedroom. The events of that morning, when Hasting's body had been discovered, played through his mind again, and this time, the events took on new meaning.

Ken got up attempting not to disturb his wife's sleep, but she rolled over, her eyes opening.

"You getting up already?" she said.

He bent over and kissed her forehead.

"Yes, it's going to be a long day. I hope to see you for lunch?" he said, confirming their earlier plans to have lunch with his father. They had agreed Bernice would bring their children along to help distract his father should the decision not go in their favor.

"Yes, I'll be there with the kids. Hope it turns out better than you are thinking it is going to," she said, her eyes once again closing.

He took a quick shower, putting on his uniform preparing for the day. He was sure he would be interviewed as the day progressed and thought looking official was important. Something else told him that wearing the uniform was going to be important today as well.

He skipped his normal cup of coffee grabbing an apple, and a coke from the refrigerator and left the house. Once in the car, he made the call back to Henry Drake. It was only 6:45 AM, but as normal, Henry answered the phone by the third ring.

"Henry, could you meet me back at the tree this morning?," Ken asked.

"Sure, when?," Henry responded, leaving the unspoken "why" hanging in the air.

"I know its early, but could you meet me there in a half hour? I think today is going to be a bit crazy, with the court decision due, and everything else, but I would like to get your insight into something I've been thinking about," Ken said.

"Sure, do I need to bring anything?," Henry asked.

"No, just you. I have an idea, but I think I need you there to shoot holes in it, in case it is wrong," Ken said.

"I'll see you there," Henry replied.

Twenty minutes later, Ken was staring up at the tree again. Five minutes after he got there, the Tree Doctor truck and Henry arrived.

Ken outlined his thoughts to Henry.

"Where there new cleat marks on the tree when you met me here the last time?," Ken asked.

Henry thought about it, and said, "I don't think I thought about that."

Together they walked closer to the tree, and Henry began examining the tree again. Finally, he pointed to a number of marks, that started about four foot up the tree trunk. There were numerous marks, some darker than others. He pointed to the lighter marks.

"Those are newer," he said.

Ken nodded.

"Can you look at the spacing of the newer marks, and give me your impression of the person who made the marks?" Ken asked.

Henry nodded, seeing where the line of questioning was going.

Henry pulled out a measuring tape from his pocket and started looking at the marks. Ten minutes later, he was done.

"I'd say the person who climbed the tree was about 5'6, maybe as tall as 5'8 and weighed between 115 and 130 pounds. He'd have to be pretty strong, to wrestle the body up the hill, as there were no drag marks as I remember, which means he carried a 150-pound dead weight, up the hill with no problems," Henry said.

"Are the new marks the same as the old marks?" Ken asked.

"I thought you might ask that question, so I measured some of the other older marks as well. They appear to be the same, so either it was the same person, or someone built incredibly like the original," Henry said.

Then Ken dropped his bomb shell, the thought that had audibly passed through his mind while lying next to his Bernice.

"You said he, Henry. Could it have been a woman, and not a man?"

Henry heard the question, looking startled.

"You mean, you think the person that did this was a woman?" Henry said.

Ken could see that the horror of what had been done to Hastings had prejudiced Henry's thoughts as well. Neither Ken, nor Henry, or any of the experts, had ever postulated the potential of the killer being a woman. They had always assumed it was a man.

Henry finally said,

"I can't rule it out, but a woman? What kind of woman could do that to anyone?", Henry asked.

"Exactly," thought Ken, what kind of woman?

Ken replayed the events of that morning, so many years ago.

The call had come into the office just after nine in the morning. The two boys had been leaving Hitchenburgh by the only road that led in and out of the town. Hitchenburgh lay just four miles from Interstate 94 that would take you to Kalamazoo, or towards Grand Rapids. The boys had wanted to spend the day to Kalamazoo, but never made it. They had seen the body hanging upside down dangling from the tree. They had called in to the sheriff's office and then waited until Ken had arrived. They both had thrown up, when they saw the brand sticking clearly out of the dead man's eye. It was reassuring to Ken that despite all of the horror movies and other bloody movies the boys had watched, seeing the results of evil close up, still was enough to rattle them. They had seen no other vehicle or people close by.

Ken had made the call to the office and to Henry. The television truck had arrived less than thirty minutes later, just before Henry had made it, and well before the medical examiner and state police crime scene investigators had made it. The news reporter said they were on the way to Hitchenburgh, to do a follow-up story of the events related to the death of Buddy House, and the destruction of the Parlor and had seen the sheriff's car stopped. Obviously, the hanging body grabbed their attention as well.

Ken had tried his hardest, to keep them away from the crime scene, and they had complied for the most part, even returning to the truck until Henry and the investigators arrived. When they had arrived, the reporter had emerged again from the truck, camera man following. What had happened next was the first experience Ken had ever had of a pushy, noisy reporter, asking lots of questions, he had no answers for. It was when the reporter had raised the specter of drugs being involved in Hitchenburgh that he had finally lost his cool. He had absolutely no knowledge of what the source of this crime had been, and he resented the question, as it appeared that the reporter knew something he did not.

The reporter and the cameraman had backed off, only to try and interview the two boys. Once again, Ken had intervened before the boys had been able to do more that answer in the affirmative that they had discovered the body. Ken had asked the reporter again to back off and give them some time to conduct the investigation.

"How did the man get here, he's not a resident of Hitchenburgh is he?" the reporter had asked again.

"He's not a resident of Hitchenburgh, that is for sure. But how he got here, I don't know, and we will issue a statement when we are further along in the investigation. Now back off please and let us do our work," Ken remembered saying.

The reporter had turned away, the cameraman in tow. Ken had watched as the reporter had taken up another position, and then told the cameraman to get rolling. Ken listened as the reporter outlined the grisly discovery, and then introduced the sheriff. Ken realized that a little fancy editing and the audience would never know that the introduction had occurred after the brief interview.

It was as the reporter and the cameraman had headed back to the truck, that Ken heard the reporter say, "I wonder if they've checked the airport. I think some private planes still land there from time to time."

It was at the airport, that Ken had discovered the murder scene, the sleek Gulfstream jet sitting unattended at the mostly abandoned airport. The small airport had been built by Buddy House, and his small fleet of jets regularly ferried him between Hitchenburgh and all of the other cities where the Parlors were popping up like chicken pox. It really was nothing more than a small building with a four-lane wide strip of asphalt that ran more than four thousand feet allowing small turbo props and smaller jets to arrive and depart. After Buddy's death, it had fallen into disrepair, and the jet sat on the pavement, already pot marked with encroaching weeds.

Ken had forgotten the comment of the reporter as being the thought that had sent him on the mission that would lead to the discovery of the jet. The jet itself was a treasure trove of evidence. But as the crime scene investigators soon confirmed, the real evidence as to who had done the crime, was missing or buried in the mountains of evidence.

Ken had discovered the trophy room, the secret panel opening up into a small room just off the bathroom in the jet. That room was barely large enough for one person to fit into. All sorts of personal affects, the matching drawers with the racks of brands, and the single cassette tape, were found. It had been obvious that the killer had known of the room as well. The crime scene investigators found the evidence that personal affects had been handled, and later it was confirmed, that every piece of clothing had the marks left by the plastic fasteners used by the dry-cleaning industry to attach the identification of ownership to each piece of clothing. All except one was missing its identification.

Every brand was numbered and there appeared to be well over 500 matched brands. Only a little over 350 personal items were found. Each drawer held twenty items, except two. The first and second drawers both held nineteen items. More than half of the stored items were masculine in nature. Ken realized that the brothers, or at least Hastings, were equal opportunity sadists. The only brands missing were the ones in the first slot at the top of the first row. Those they had found, one buried within Hastings' eye, the other on top of the cassette tape. The tape was well over an hour in length, and it detailed the suffering that Hasting's had gone through.

Then only personal affect with any identification still attached, rested in the last drawer, and in the last position. The expensive brazier was red, and it barely disguised its intended use. This brazier was to display not hide or support a woman's breasts. The name had caused Ken's jaw to drop open. It was immediately obvious that the killer had desired the name to be known.

Strangely, that morning a verse had shattered his attempt to go back to sleep.

"The first will be last," had echoed in his mind.

What if that brazier had been in the first position, and had been moved by the killer, to the last drawer, with the name still attached to it. The killer wanted that person to be found, to be embarrassed by all the questions related to being attached to the brothers.

The DNA lab had been busy for almost a year, processing all of the evidence. Amazingly, only two DNA samples ever led to any identification. One was a state senator from California, who had committed suicide more than ten years earlier; the other was a nurse from a VA hospital in Oklahoma.

She had been caught up in a drug ring and had spent over twelve years in a federal prison for her part in smuggling in drugs in the bodies of dead soldiers. She refused any comment on her connections with Hastings or Avery Moment.

"I've paid my dues for my crime, go away, I am not talking to you or anyone else about those two creeps," was all she would say. There was nothing that anyone could do at this point, as the current evidence pointed to her more as a victim than a criminal. After everything, the only evidence pointing to anyone known, was the name attached to that brazier.

Ken had approached that person. She had shown up at the service where his father had started the process of trying to cope with the prior pastor's sins. In the end, her story checked out, as her two children were waiting for her, for one of her random visits to Hitchenburgh. He never shared the discovery of her name on the item. At the time, her name had jumped to the top of his list as a suspect, but he had quickly been able to confirm that there was no way she could have been the murderer. There was plenty of evidence that she was in Washington DC and was just days away from her new marriage. No, her name had definitely been a plant, left there to bring embarrassment. But now it was clear, this was more than just embarrassment in mind, if she really had been in the number one position, what would that mean.

That strange question, thrown at her by the reporter, which she had artfully danced around, something about being number one, again, recorded on the tape the two deputies had made.

Ken looked back at his friend.

'Thanks Henry, you have helped me crack the case, I think," Ken said.

"Okay, that's great, who did it?" Henry asked, baffled that something he had said had solved the case. If it had been a game of clue, Ken was sure he would have laid all his cards on the table with his friend.

"Can't tell you yet, Henry, but maybe in the next day or so, you'll know," Ken said.

Ken saw his friends face, screwing up to say something else, but then falling still.

'I promise, Henry, as soon as I can, I will tell you," patting his friend on his shoulder as they headed back to their vehicles.

Ken entered his fathers' house twenty minutes later. It was just a little after eight AM. Buddy House was sitting with his father watching the small television that was resting on the counter in the kitchen. It was funny for Ken, to see the person who had at one time been the richest person in the state, sitting in this modest house with his father, watching a small, out of date television.

"Hey son, you're here a little sooner than you said you would be," his father said.

"Came to talk to Buddy and thought I would catch you both before I go to the office," Ken said.

At the same time, a voice came on the television.

"We interrupt this show to bring you breaking news from our Washington DC bureau," the voice said.

All three men turned to watch.

They watched as a woman was being handcuffed and placed in the back of a black Chevy Suburban government vehicle. The woman was wearing gym clothes, as if she had been preparing for a normal morning run or exercise routine. All three men gasped, as they recognized the woman. A reporter's voice was heard narrating the scene that was unfolding.

"We have learned that Kristin Rosewood, wife of Senator Rosewood who is also the new Vice Presidential nominee for his party, is being arrested for tax evasion and conspiracy to commit fraud, we have not learned where she is being taking for holding and arrangement, but we have learned that Senator Rosewood is apparently not under indictment and is not considered a suspect in his wife's crimes, but needless to say, this calls into question the announcement made only two days ago, of his ascendency to the vice presidential slot.

The early morning arrest was made by treasury and FBI agents who we are told have been conducting a multiyear investigation into Mrs. Rosewood's activities. Why the government allowed her husband to take the role on, only to have this humiliating incident ending almost certainly his candidacy, we don't know, but we do know that the Senator was called to the White House for an early morning meeting. We are sure, it has to do with the unfolding events. We tried to reach the senators' campaign manager, but his team seems to be in disarray over the unfolding events, and we were unable to get any comment. We will keep you alerted as developments happen throughout the day. This is Peg Ryan reporting for TV4 in Washington, DC."

A red head reporter with a slightly crooked mouth, as if she had suffered from a stroke or other injury, signed off, her smile seemingly out of place for the events that had just unfolded.

"My wife's in trouble," Buddy said, forgetting that Kristin had not been his wife for a number of years, and that she thought she had killed him.

"More trouble than you know," said Ken, looking at the seemingly frozen picture of Peg Ryan on the screen. Peg Ryan, the reporter who was first on the scene, the reporter who had dropped the seemingly overheard comment about the plane.

"What kind of woman... ", Ken thought.

"Buddy, what do you know about the reporter, Peg Ryan?" Ken asked.

"Peg?" Buddy asked.

Chapter 10 – Exposure

Kristin slipped into the hot tub full of water. She felt so dirty, she swore she would soak in the tub until the water was ice cold, and then she turned the hot water on to a slow dribble, to make sure that the water would never get cold. For twelve hours she had lived liked a caged animal, fighting for her life. She couldn't believe everything that had happened, but in the end, even with everything going against her, she had emerged triumphant. Her planning and determination had paid off.

As she thought about the hours and all that had been lost, her anger continued to grow. She was going to get even, and she ticked off in her mind, just who was going to pay. They thought they had gotten the best of her, but now it was her turn. She would make them regret the day they thought to take her on. Especially Jim, she was angry the most with him. She allowed her near photographic memory replay what she had gone through.

After Jim's strange behavior, and her unsettling nightmare, Kristin finally slipped back into sleep. Her alarm woke her, the first time in months that it needed to do so. She got out of bed and walked to the master bedroom. The door was open, and Jim was already gone. She looked at the clock. 7:00 AM shone brightly back at her. There was no note at the front door, so Jim must still be upset. Well, she wasn't going to allow that to concern her too much. Her mind slipped back again to the triumphs at the reception. Whatever was bothering Jim, didn't come close to the success that he would get to share coming out of the reception.

She looked at the clock again. Earl would be downstairs in fifteen minutes, ready to take her back to the health club and in time for her to burn off some of the rich food and drinks from the reception. She decided she would need to run a few miles on the treadmill, and then perhaps she'd ride a few miles on the bike before she hit the sauna there, that had been her cover yesterday. This time, she would really enjoy it.

She slipped into her exercise outfit, this time a much more modest, normal set of shorts and shirt that she covered with the longer set of workout pants and then the teal blue zip up cover. She picked out a set of clothes and shoes for the day, putting them in her gym bag, and headed for the door. After she excised, she would see if she could find where Jim had gone, and then she would see if she could snap him back into the type of mood he should be in. And if she couldn't find him, well then, she would grab a bite with some of her friends. There were many just waiting for her to call, to let them know it was their day to have good fortune. Or maybe the general would be available for lunch? The potentials were endless.

As normal there was a secret service agent waiting for her, just outside the door. She hadn't seen this one before, he was an older man, but still muscled in ways that only highly trained men were. He also was dressed in the mandatory black suit, with a white shirt and blue tie, and he had the ear piece that seemed to shout...look at me, I'm a secret agent man! For a moment, she thought there was something familiar about him, but then they all looked alike.

"Do you know where my husband went this morning?" she asked curtly, already striding to the elevator.

'Yes, maam, he had an appointment with the President, he is over at the White House I believe," the agent said.

They road in silence to the ground floor. The agent followed her out the door. Outside there were the normal large black Chevy Suburban, but this time three of them stood in a row, but Earl and his limo were no were to be seen.

"Where's Earl?" she said, her vexation growing.

At that same moment one of the doors on the closest Suburban's opened, and she saw motion to her side. She saw the reporter, the television camera, and felt the agent behind her slipping close to her.

"Mrs. Rosewood, I have a warrant for your arrest," the agent said, at the same time Kristin felt the handcuff snap around her one wrist, followed by a jerking motion as her other arm was quickly restrained and the other handcuff snapped into place. She had dropped her gym bag, as the agent had grabbed her other wrist. The agent half pushed her into the car, where Kristin discovered another agent was waiting for her. The agent behind her was still talking, giving her rights, the whole time she could hear as well, the reporter speaking about what was occurring. Kristin looked at the reporter, just before the car door closed. It was that red head reporter, the same one that had asked that question that ruined her first audience, and the same one whose passing inclusion in the photo at the Grill had caught Kristin's attention before her meeting with Avery.

The car was already moving before the agent had finished his spiel.

"I want my attorney," were the first words out of Kristin's mouth.

She turned looking at the agent who had been sitting in the car, waiting for her arrival. He had a broad smile, and she instantly recognized this man.

"Agent Smither's, to what do I owe the pleasure of meeting you again?" Kristin said. The memory of her dying husband, and the absolute tizzy Agent Smither was in, prior to Jim arriving and help calm the whole situation down. He had been the agent that Buddy had cut the deal with, to go into hiding from the brothers. He had been the most insistent of all the agents that the house be searched from top to bottom, and he was the one who seemed to have the greatest difficulty believing Kristin's story. In the end, Jim Rosewood had won, and despite the agent's protests, the court had released Kristin into Jim's care. Two years later, she and Jim were married, and on their way to the White House.

"Do you know what you are doing?" was Kristin's second question.

"Yes, I know exactly what I am doing" he replied.

"I've been waiting for this moment for a long time. Perhaps you didn't hear what Doug told you, but you are under arrest for tax evasion and conspiracy to commit fraud, and if I had my way, I would be charging you with a host of other things, but for the time being tax evasion and conspiracy is a good start" he said.

His look was one of smug satisfaction. Kristin chose not to respond, her mind already outlining what was going to need to happen. She knew what she was in for, and what she was going to do about it.

They arrived at the federal building in less than ten minutes, and the car zipped right past the security station and into the private garage. Fortunately, there were no additional news people here, the one at her home had more than enough. Kristin wondered how she had learned of the arrest. If it had been public, there would have been way more, than just her. And why her?

Kristin chose to stay silent, until she was ushered into a room with a table and four chairs. Doug, who Kristin now remembered as the quiet sulking partner of Agent Smithers, pulled one of the chairs out, and pushed her into it.

"I want my lawyer, and I want a phone, and I want these cuffs off me, now. You better get ready, because when I'm done with you, you're not going to be able to sit down for a week, and you will be looking for a new career, and I am going to make sure you never find one," Kristin stated.

"Mrs. Rosewood, unfortunately for you, you don't get to call the shots at this point. I do. But you will have your lawyer, and your phone call, when I'm ready to allow that. In the meantime, make yourself comfortable. You're going to be here for a while," Agent Smithers said.

Both agents left her, still handcuffed, seated. It was more than ten minutes before Agent Smithers returned. Kristin knew the tactic. They were trying to crack her, thinking her veneer was not as thick as she knew it was. He finally released her hands, taking the cuffs off. And so, it began, the tug of war.

She finally had gotten her calls. The first call had been to her attorney, who she had directed to also get a hold of the accountant and make it down to her. Her second call was to her husband. Jim didn't answer, but the phone's answering machine did.

"Jim don't do anything stupid. There's no truth to the allegations, and by the end of the day, they are going to wish they had never done something as dumb as this. If you just hang in there, I will get this cleared up quickly, and you and I will be right back where we were, before this happened," Kristin said, suppressing what she really was going to say to Jim, when this was over. But for the time being, she needed to get Jim back into a frame of mind that focused on the future he wanted, almost as much as she did.

Her third call was to the Agent Smithers' boss. She smiled to herself after the conversation. Agent Smither was about to discover an orifice he didn't know he possessed earlier in the day.

The agents had stripped her of her blackberry, but she didn't need it. Her memory for phone numbers and names, was nearly as good as the electronic gadget. Besides the real power was in the tapes, safely secured back at her office. But the blackberry did have some information Kristin did not want the agents to get, but she had encrypted the device and had a special security item on it as well. Her fourth call was too a special number and when it did not answer immediately, she entered the code, and she could almost hear the shouts of the agents as the device erased and then melted the chip. Nothing like being a step ahead, she told herself, and all from the comfort of their little cell.

Kristin knew that the feeding frenzy of the press was probably at fever pitch. She also suspected that her wayward husband had somehow gotten the news that she was in trouble, and he had abandoned her, leaving her to fend for herself. She was also sure that he thought his lofty goals for his career were over, but Jim didn't know, what Kristin knew. If he just would wait, not only would they ride out this storm, but she would turn this storm into a public triumph.

Kristin never had to go in front of a judge. By six o'clock that evening, not only had Agent Smithers' case disappeared, but all of the backup to the fact that Kristin had in fact paid all of her taxes, had in fact sold the supposed hidden business to Avery Moment immediately after the death of Hastings, and had in fact been falsely accused magically appeared. She had written out exactly the apology Agent Smithers' boss was going to deliver to the news media.

Her attorneys had already filed a lawsuit against the agency, against the agents, and against the rival party, which their complaint alleged would be shown to be at the bottom of this most grievous miscarriage of justice.

When she finally emerged from the federal building flanked by several of her lawyers the mob of reporters was larger than anything she had ever seen before. Questions were flying around her like angry bees, but during those questions, she heard the one thing she had feared the most. Her stupid husband had not waited, he had gone ahead and announced his withdrawal from the race, "for the good of the president and the party," even before she had finally been allowed to make her calls.

"That stupid whimp!" Kristin mind shouted out.

Kristin felt her body heat increasing, her anger building.

She turned off the hot water, she was plenty hot enough. They were all going to pay, but especially her stupid husband. She got out of the water, wrapped the terry cloth bathrobe around herself, and headed for her office.

She had planning to do. This wasn't over yet.

She turned on the computer and saw the flashing file, indicating a new uploaded file.

"What the heck is this?," she thought.

Clicking on the file, the video and sound immediately emerged. It was a woman, straddling a man. Kristin watched mesmerized. The woman's red hair bounced freely, the man's face hidden, but his voice instantly recognizable.

"My God Pam, you're incredible, better than she ever was" the man said.

The woman turned, her face clear in the picture, and smiled upwards, the slightly crooked smile still revealing the damage. It was obvious she knew that she was being watched.

She turned back to the man, 'Go ahead Jim, say it again, just for me," her voice urging as her motion intensified.

"You're my number one everything I have ever wanted, you are," Jim's voice strangely contorted as he reached a conclusion.

The tape continued and continued and continued. The woman finally turned in all her nakedness and stared up at the camera, she slowly got off the naked man on the bed and moved a chair into place, smiled at the camera again, and then the tape stopped. There was no doubt, that was Jim on the bed.

When it finished, Kristin looked at the time. They had been at it for almost an hour before the woman had stopped and disabled the camera. Kristin looked at the date and time stamp. She felt her anger growing even hotter. When she had called her husband, to tell him not to do anything stupid, they had been here. He had already done the stupid thing she was afraid of, but here he was, while she had been fighting for everything they had wanted, Jim and Pam had been here breaking her one cardinal rule.

Kristin got up and walked to the master bedroom. The room was a mess. The activities recorded, amply displayed. The damaged camera unveiled was dangling from where it had been hidden. She saw the note on the dresser, sitting on a crumpled pair of red laced underwear.

"I'm his number one. Oh, I'm borrowing your files, it's your move now my dearie."

Kristin froze. The last two words, "My Dearie" she had heard those words from only one source. The voice, that had shared in so many of her successes, and that had so suddenly disappeared. Kristin returned quickly to her office. It was gone. The only file still on her computer was the latest one. The secure storage file, and everything on it, was gone.

For only the second time in her life, Kristin was lost. Anger welled up, but with it a sense of impending doom. Her files that were the source of her power, were gone. She stared at the screen, and hit the replay button again, watching her husband and Pam reenact everything. It was worse for Kristin the second time around and did not improve with the third. It was hours before Kristin went to bed, and for the first time in her life, she didn't have a plan. That fact ensured, she would not sleep at all, as her mind refused all attempts to be turned off.

CHAPTER 11 – RULINGS AND CONSEQUENCES

The ruling came in right at 1:00 PM. The phone had rung less than five minutes later, and the message was delivered by an attorney Ken did not know. They had put the phone on speaker mode, and everyone in the room heard about the judgment at the same time.

"Pastor Farr, this is Bob Gibson from Taylor Whilte and Blthye. I believe you are with the elders of First Presbyterian there, is that correct?"

"Yes, they are here with me," Ken's father responded.

"I have David Wayne of the Northeastern Presbytery on the line with us as well," continued the lawyer.

"Gentlemen, the Michigan Supreme Court ruling on our case has been given, and I am afraid to say, that while they have clarified several parts of the original decision, they have mostly left in place the findings of the lower court. We are of course unhappy with the result and based on our earlier discussions with both David and the elders at the church we are preparing the next filing that will move this from the state court system into the federal system. We have confirmed our intent with the state court, and they have agreed to hold on the execution of the findings of the court until we see whether we are successful in raising this case with the federal system. I wish I had better news for you, but at this point that is where we are. We expect it will take another six months before we will know whether our filings with the federal courts are accepted. My suspicion is that if they are accepted, this case will end up before the Supreme Court within three years. So, the fight continues, but at this point frankly, the cards are stacked against us."

Despite the news, that Ken's father had seemed to almost prophetically predict, there was jubilation in Ken's father's home. So strange, that despite the adverse ruling from the Michigan Supreme Court, that had just been delivered by phone call, there was so much joy in the large group of people crowded into the home.

As Ken had planned Bernice arrived with their children at their grandfathers' home just before lunch. The home already was packed, with both Jeffery and Martha Day, along with their daughter Theresa and her fiancée Scott Brown standing in the living room. Theresa's son Jonathan stood beside her, now six years old, but still tethered to the oxygen tank he needed, as he continued to struggle with cystic fibrous. Despite his own struggles, her son was constantly smiling, and Ken knew that Scott loved Jonathan as if he was his own son.

Also crammed into the room, were several other elders from the church, as well as Glenn Hitch, Jim House, Susan House, and amazingly Buddy House. The source of the joy in the room though was the arrival of another young woman that now sat beside her parents. At 12:30 PM, as Ken and Bernice were carrying the trays of sandwiches they had made, to feed the folks that had come by to show their support for Pastor Jerry Farr, there was a light rapping on the front door. Glenn had stood up and walked to the door.

Ken saw Glenn's face as he heard the knock. It was as if he'd been waiting for that knock, as a smile split his face even before he opened the door. He had opened the door wide, inviting the person in, even as every eye turned in the room to see who the new arrival was.

Alison Day entered the room, a suit case in one hand, and a white handled carrier in the other. Silence reigned in the room. It was broken by Alison's mother Martha, who had stood and walked quickly to her daughter. Ken remembered that Alison had appeared to brace herself, expecting her mother to slap her, or push her, or do something to indicate her displeasure at seeing her. Instead Martha had thrown her arms around Alison.

"Alison, thank God you're okay. Forgive us honey, please forgive us!", Martha's words tumbling out and tears flowing down her face.

Alison's father Jeffery had joined his wife, and now his arms were around both his daughter and his wife, his words mirroring his wife's.

"Thank you, Lord! Oh Alison, we are so sorry," Jeffery said bursting into tears as well.

Alison began to sob, her knees buckling, and her head resting on her mother's shoulder.

'Mom, Dad, I'm the one who needs forgiving. I was sure you would never want to see me again. But I just had nowhere else to go," Alison said.

At that moment a small cry emerged from the blankets covering the white carrier that Alison still clung to. Still weeping Alison put the carrier down and uncovered the infant whose crying was increasing in volume. Jonathan, oxygen bottle in one hand, came over and took the handle of the suit case from Alison.

"Aunt Alison, let me take the suit case for you," Jonathan said.

Alison had picked up the infant, who was dressed in a pink sleeper, and wiggled while still crying. She released her hold on the suitcase and watched as Jonathan hauled it into the living room. It was then that Theresa had joined her parents as well.

"That's your son?" Alison asked, when Theresa was close.

'Yes, that's Jonathan," Theresa answered.

Ken knew that Alison had never met Jonathan before. She had been gone for almost five years, and before that, none of the Day's had taken any interest in Jonathan.

"And this must be Mary," Theresa said, taking the crying infant from her sister.

"Yes, this is Mary, Alison confirmed.

Over the next hour, Alison told her story, and had just reached a lull when the phone had rung with the call from the attorney. Despite that news, the presence of Theresa and Mary had made the announcement of the loss almost inconsequential. It was Alison who reacted first.

"Kevin is probably dancing in the street for joy," she said, her voice bitter and angry.

"He maybe be, but he lost something far greater than this minor victory. He lost you and your daughter!" the words coming from Ken's father. Everyone looked at Pastor Farr, and then back to Theresa.

"I don't think he thinks of it as a loss, Pastor, you see, he already has someone else in his life. So, I don't think my leaving he even considers a minor inconvenience, in fact he probably thinks it could not have worked out better. When he discovered I was pregnant with Mary, he changed, or I finally got to see the real him. He wanted me to get an abortion, saying that he already had all the children he needed or wanted. I knew about his children, but I thought for sure that when he said he loved me, that he would love our children as well. But I was wrong.

It was also when I discovered the truth about Jonathan. In one of his rants, he said: 'You are just like your sister, I should have figured you would not know what is best.' It was at that moment I understood that Kevin was Jonathan's father as well. I didn't know what to say, I was so shell shocked. I always thought that someone else was Jonathan's father," Alison said, looking squarely at Buddy House, who everyone in the room knew was the person the town had suspect as being the absentee father.

Buddy just nodded. He had heard the allegations, but he knew that they were wrong. Despite everything he had done, he had not slept with Theresa. But he knew his reputation preceded him, and his past gave the suspicion the legs it needed. It was exactly the rumor that Pastor Kevin Hill had spread, covering his own role even further. That rumor had come close to destroying Alison, and certainly had damaged her reputation and the reputation of the infant, now a young child, to the point that even her parents had disowned her, only to discover the horrible truth when their second daughter had run off with the wayward pastor.

"When I refused to get an abortion our relationship began to fall apart. Two months before Mary was born, I caught him with another woman, in our bed. He pushed me out of the bedroom and slammed thedoor. They were in there for another hour. I know, because I sat on the couch crying and waiting. When she finally left, he went with her. For the last three months, I've only seen him sporadically. Of course, he's still preaching at his church, but I stopped going, and his new mistress sits right up there in the front row anyway. Everyone knows what they're doing, and no one cares, and no one there cared about me, or about Mary. If it hadn't been for Glenn, I probably would have killed myself."

Every eye in the room had turned to Glenn, as up to now, Alison's story had not mentioned Glenn, or his involvement.

"Glenn was there?" Ken asked, broaching the question that he was sure was on everyone else's mind as well.

Alison looked at Glenn, the worried look that perhaps she had revealed something she should not have flashing across the distance, but Glenn simply nodded, giving Alison both relief and permission to answer the question.

'Yes, after Kevin left with his new woman, I was a wreck. I thought about killing myself right then and there. I wanted to do something that would hurt Kevin, or at least cause him some problems with his new friends. I had just figured out what I was going to do when Glenn knocked on my door.

'Alison, killing yourself would not solve anything, and there are others that love you and want you back, both you and your daughter.' Not "hi, you may not remember me, but I am Glenn Hitch from Hitchenburgh, but instead he hit me with what I had been thinking about, as if he had been in my head. I just stood there, shell shocked. I hadn't told anyone about Mary, I mean, about the child being a girl. I thought only the nurse and I knew that fact. But then I saw Glenn's friends, and well, I understood how he knew and why he was there."

"Glenn's friends?" Ken asked, already knowing the answer, but needing a confirmation that Alison had seen what he suspected she had.

Once again, Alison looked towards Glenn, again the obvious fear that she had gone too far flashing across her face. But once again, Glenn just smiled and nodded.

"Yes, the two angels were behind him at the door. When I invited Glenn in, they just faded out. When I turned around, after Glenn passed by me, they were standing in the living room, waiting for us."

Alison's story took another hour to finish. She spoke about Mary's birth, the fact that only Glenn was there and had made sure she had gotten to the hospital and then had helped care for her and Mary for the two weeks after the birth. Glenn had told her finally, 'It's time you go home. You need your family and they need you." That had been yesterday, and here she was.

Now Glenn's disappearance, and the weeks he had been away made sense. As did his obvious joy at hearing the knock at the door. Ken wondered how much more there was to the story, but he kept his questions to himself.

At four in the afternoon the group had begun to disperse. The Days, with Alison and Mary, along with Scott Brown, Theresa and Jonathan were the first to leave. They were followed shortly thereafter by the other elders from the church, and then Bernice and Ken's children left.

Buddy's children, Jim and Susan stood to leave as well Both Jim and Buddy asked Glenn and Ken about Jim's graduation that would occur just three days away, on Saturday. Buddy had been invited, and he wanted Ken to go with him. Ken readily agreed. It was Jim's question though to Glenn that got Ken's attention.

"Glenn, do you know whether my mom is going to come to the graduation?" Jim had asked. Jim's face was full of expectation and hope.

Ken understood the question. Based on what Alison had just shared, it was a logical question. If Glenn had known that Alison was thinking about killing herself, and that the unborn child was a girl, then it was a logical assumption that he might also know the answer to this question as well.

Glenn only shook his head.

"I don't know. And just so you know, I didn't know what Alison was thinking. I was told what Alison was thinking," he said.

It sounded like a contradiction, but Ken understood immediately what

Glenn had just said. The awareness of what Alison was contemplating was not something Glenn had insight in by himself. Instead, he had been told what she had been thinking.

But then Glenn continued, "But, I suspect she will be there. Things are coming to a head for her as well. You and Susan are family, and where else do you head when things are going badly?"

That made sense to both Jim and Susan.

Finally, Ken stood, hugged his father and shook Buddy's hand. He just smiled at Glenn.

"Dad, can we do a late dinner tomorrow, I have some more questions I need to ask you," Ken asked.

"Sure Son, what time do you have in mind," His father asked. 'Say about 8:30 PM, I'll pick you up.'

Ken's father nodded.

As Ken passed through the door, the thoughts about what was likely waiting for him at the office were interrupted by Buddy's question to Glenn,

"What about Kristin?"

The door closed, before Ken could hear Glenn's response.

CHAPTER 12 – GRADUATION CONFRONTATION

Ken watched the graduation from the back of the temporary stand that had been set up for the occasion. It had taken a day to get all the tickets and other arrangements completed. The discovery of the true paternity for Jim House had changed a lot of things. Jim, the person who should have been most upset by the discovery, was taking the revelation in stride. Jim had even made the changes to allow his step brother and his newly discovered family to attend the graduation. Even more startling was his invitation to Jenny Housher to attend and exceeding even that washer acceptance.

But what was most amazing was the relationship developing between Buddy and Jim. The discovery that Buddy was not Jim's father seemed to free both men from much of the baggage from the past. Buddy was true to his word, and had been acting more like Jim's father, than he had ever acted when he was unaware of Jim's true parentage. Even Buddy was invited to the graduation, and he too had agreed to come. Buddy had asked that Ken accompany him, and that he be allowed to sit in the back, away from Julie Housher and from John Housher, as the relationship with that family still had a long way to go.

The small Christian School sat atop a mountain known as Lookout Mountain, in Tennessee. The scenery was brilliant with the panorama of the valley beneath the school laid out before them. It seemed more than appropriate for the graduation to be outside, as the day was bright and colorful, and the vista was breathtaking. With only two hundred potential graduates, there were still several thousand people in attendance. Ken marveled at the ratio and wondered how many other graduations would be as well attended.

It was just before the ceremony was to begin that he saw the limousine pull up to the drop off point for the people attending the ceremony, and there she was. Even from this distance Ken recognized Kristin Rosewood as she exited the back of the car. Buddy, standing next to Ken in the crowd, stiffened, so Ken knew Buddy saw her as well.

Kristin handed the young woman guarding the entrance to the grounds an envelope. That caused a stir and Ken watched amused as the woman conferred with others before turning back to Kristin. Even from this distance Ken could see the impatience building in Kristin's stance,and he could guess the exchange that was taking place. Kristin was not accustomed to waiting for anyone. Finally, Kristin had stood aside allowing others that had arrived behind her to enter the venue, while one of the ushers that had conferred with the woman at the entrance went running.

About five minutes later Ken watched as Jim House, in full cap and gown, followed the usher back to where his mother stood. Jim did something that surprised Ken, he threw his arms around his mother,giving her an embrace. Ken watched as Kristin's body went from the rigid posture it had taken, to a much more relaxed form, and then Jim had led his mother to a seat, much further up in the audience, but still away from Julie Housher and John Housher.

Ken felt Buddy relax, and he turned to look at Buddy. Buddy's face was glowing, and tears were streaming down his face.

"Jim is quite a man," Buddy said, wiping at his eyes with the handkerchief from his pocket.

In those few words, Ken experienced the change that had occurred in Buddy. He certainly was no longer the Buddy of old.

The ceremony was typical of most graduation ceremonies, and the order of the events were readily understood and well-orchestrated. It was when the president of the college made the announcement of the Valedictorian and called on Jim House to give his speech that Ken felt tension building again.

Jim shook the president's hand and then took his spot at the lectern."President Jeremiah, distinguished guests, parents, family members, and my fellow graduates, well we've made it!"

Laughter from the graduates and some in the audience followed by some clapping flowed around Ken. Jim waited briefly and then continued.

"I believe that I can speak for all of the graduates when I tell you of our profound gratitude to all who have worked so long and hard to make this day possible for us," a ripple of applause accompanied this,primarily through the two hundred graduates seated immediately in front of the stage.

"It is normal for the valedictorian to take this time to speak of the accomplishments of the past four years, and look ahead to the time immediately before us and to challenge us as a class related to the future. I will not deviate too much from that time-honored tradition.

My father told my brother, before I was born, that it would never be the work, it would always be the people, that would make his life challenging. I never knew my father, as he died before I was born,but I have learned that he was profoundly wise, and his words were true. During our four years together, I think it is fair to say that one of the major accomplishments for us as a class, is we learned how to work together,without killing one another."

Laughter erupted among the graduates and Ken heard one graduate call out, "Were not out of here yet, Jim."

More laughter, but it was clear that the graduates all respected Jim,and the banter was light hearted, although Ken was surprised by it. Ken looked over to where Kristin was sitting. From this angle he could not tell how she had taken the revelation that Jim knew his real father was not Buddy House and that he knew he had a brother. Jim continued, smiling but un-phased by the interruption.

"We learned that we as people are complex beings, that while we share much in common, that each of us are truly unique. Like our fingerprints,we each have unique qualities, strengths, and weaknesses that do not fully define us, but certainly serve as some of the things we have to offer to each other. It's when you put all the uniqueness together, that you really seethe strength of this class.

When one was weak, another was strong, and together we were far more than what anyone of us would have been alone. The world will tell us, leave the weak behind, as it is the survival of the fittest. But we learned that often it was the weak one that knew how to start a fire, or who knew how to strain the poison out of the berries so that we could eat them,or the one that knew where the water was. I think as a class we learned that those, whose weaknesses were obvious, often had strengths that were hidden and even more needed; while those of us with obvious strength soften had far greater debilitating weaknesses that would manifest at the worst possible times. That understanding made this class truly unique and wonderful.

The benefit of going to such a small school, is that we all got to know one another. We had to, as we were constantly bumping into one another. I have the bruises to prove that! " Laughter again flowed through the graduates.

"We discovered a lot about each other in those interactions. I learned that each of us in this class have gifts that if used will make an impact on the world around us. The challenge for each of us is what are we going to do, with what we have been given?

What really surprised me was the realization of that fact. So much of what we are, we have been given, we didn't earn it, we were blessed with it. We do nothing to get our fingerprints, we are born with them. Many of my friends asked me how come learning was so much easier for me, than for them. I realized something early on, it wasn't anything I had done, but it was something I was given. I didn't earn it. I may have exercised my gifts but in the end, I was blessed by what I was given. Most of you don't know my mom, but she has an IQ of something like 186. I was blessed that she is my mom, as some of her is in me, making me who I am. I didn't earn that. I was blessed with it.

When I look out at all the graduates of this class, I see the same thing. Each of us has been given many gifts. Some have had to work harder than I, to get the grades they did. But some of you sing better than I ever will, and others play music far better than I do, while still others can cook,others the ability to write, and still others are better athletes, far more gifted orators, and some have been given gentle spirits that humble me when I am in their presence.

That doesn't mean we all haven't had to work for what we have accomplished, but much of our accomplishments were achieved by using well what we have been given. If we understand that, that we are simply developing and using what we have been given, then this class will go far as we leave from here.

I believe that our world today needs what this class has to offer. The world needs each of us, and our unique gifts, to help the world to be a better place. I come from a farming community. There, you learn that plowing is a difficult task, even with all the modern equipment. I worked with my grandfather, and I got to walk behind the plow picking up the stones the field seemed to yield every year. The reality is that the ground seems to produce new stones every year, stones that must be removed, if the crop is to be as good as it could be. I spent many summers with my grandfather, out on the farm clearing those rocks. I learned how hard the work was, to prepare the field every year for the planting that was to occur.

As we all head out to the next adventure in our lives, we are heading out to a world with lots of stones that need to be removed. Fifty years from now when we look back, I hope we see many fields that were once littered with stones, cleared and producing crops that are feeding many.

The time we have in this life, is also a gift. We didn't ask to be born at this time, we didn't participate in the decision of who our parents would be, who are brothers and sisters would be, which friends we would meet and make here. We call this providence and the question before all of us, is what will we make with the providence we have been given?

Most of us hope, that we will have many years yet, that we will be hereto look back at the passing fifty years but none of us know just how many years we do have. Early on in my time here, I met Jacob Smith. Some of you never got to know Jacob, most of you remember that he died in our sophomore year. What amazed me about Jacob is he came to school,knowing that he would likely never graduate. He was my roommate for the first two years of my schooling here and if he had lived, he would have likely been standing on this stage instead of me.

When I asked him why he would come to school knowing how few days he had left, he asked me, what I would do if I knew I had but a few days left. That floored me, but it forced me to think. Then he said something that really changed my life. He said, 'Jim, you only have a few days more than I do left, make the most of every day'. In the end Jacob was a light to me, as he lived everyday here, like it was his last, and like he was going to be here forever. He poured everything he had, into every day he was given. He was constantly amazed, constantly excited by what he was learning. He shared more about what it means to make the most out of the providence we are given, than any book, or professor ever could.

He reminded me of our Lord, who walked the earth for precious few years, but changed everything with the life he led, and the death he embraced, and the grave he shattered.

Each of us are called to a mission. I believe mine will take me to further schooling, and I hope eventually into the ministry where I can share what God has done for me, and too me. Regardless of whether we end up in the work place, in the military, raising a family, or multiple callings, our mission is to clear the fields so that those that come after us,can advance further than we have.

What have we accomplished? We made it this far!

What does this time need? Us, all of us.

What does the future hold for us? I don't know, but I believe we should all look forward to it and make the best of every day we are given with the desire to leave it better off than when we entered it. May we not be put to shame as we look back at our lives, but instead, let us have the great blessing of hearing, well done, my good and faithful servant. It is my hope, that God will bless each of us as we leave from here. I have confidence that he will, because you see, he already has."

Jim turned to the president of the college who stood and came forward to shake his hand. Ken had not been sure what to expect, but when the clapping started, it came from the graduates first, and soon the crowd was standing and clapping. Ken stood clapping as well, and he turned again to see what Kristin was doing, but she was no longer in her seat. Finally, he found her. She was already near the exit. She wasn't going to wait for the actual graduation.

That was when he realized that Buddy wasn't beside him any more either. He was startled that he had not realized that Buddy had left. He could not find him anywhere. He saw Kristin's limo pull up to the entrance, it had obviously been summoned, even as she reached the exit. Ken moved as quickly as he could down the row, excusing himself around the other parents that were still standing and clapping. It took him only a few minutes to make the exit, but he fully expected the limo to have left, before he got there. Surprisingly it was still there. The door on the other side of the car opened, and Buddy House appeared. The car began moving before the door was even closed, and the gravel kicked up by the car pelted Buddy. Ken experienced the rain of gravel as he arrived seconds after the car speed out of the lot.

Buddy just stood watching the retreating car.

"Buddy what did you do?" Ken asked.

Buddy turned to Ken, and Ken saw his face flushed with sadness.

"I knew she wasn't going to stay. What Jim was talking about sounds like foolishness to someone without ears to hear. I know, because it took two bullets and my supposedly dead brother to wake me up. I was hoping that perhaps if she knew that I was still alive, that it might shake her enough to cause her to want to stay and learn more about what Jim was talking about."

"Did you give her the package?" Glenn's voice startled Ken, and he turned to see Glenn with his staff standing just behind him.

"Yes, I told her what you had said, but I don't know if she believed me or not," Buddy said.

Ken looked back at Glenn, wondering about the package, but at the same time also wondering about how long Glenn had been here. Ken had not seen Glenn and did not know whether he had been invited or had come because of the business with Buddy and Kristin. Ken looked around wondering if Glenn's constant companions were also close by but saw no sign of either angel.

"You've done what you can Buddy, now all that is left is to be praying for her. Hopefully something will open her eyes, before it is too late. She is about to experience the reality of what the other side really has in store for those who think they are friendly to them. Those beings only desire to consume what light still emanates from us, even in our fallen estate. Their goal is never ending misery for us, but in this life, we often think that sin that brings pleasure has no other consequence," Glenn said.

"What happens next?" Buddy asked.

"We wait, and pray, and hope."

It didn't feel near enough for Ken, and he was about to say something when he saw Susan House approach.

"Where did mom go?", she asked.

Buddy turned, facing Susan.

"She's going back to D.C. She has some unfinished business there,"Buddy said.

Taking her hand, he turned her back to the graduation.

"Come on, let's go see your brother graduate! he said.

Together Buddy and Susan made their way back to the graduation. "What's going to happen to Kristin?" Ken asked Glenn as soon as Buddy and Susan were out of earshot.

"She's going to learn the truth," Glenn said.

CHAPTER 13 – REPLAY

It took the flight attendant way too long to bring back her first drink. Sitting in first class had many perks, but today the free drinks were a major plus. Kristin downed the cranberry laced vodka in a single gulp and had already ordered a second.

Buddy House was alive.

That fact alone had shattered her otherwise unflappable composure. It all made sense now. Obviously, Buddy had turned the IRS onto her hidden funds. He probably was behind getting that annoying reporter on to her as well. Kristin remembered seeing the reporter with Buddy on any number of occasions prior to his supposed death. She had assumed that she was just another of Buddy's conquests. As normal Buddy had been blind to the fact that his wife had known all along about Buddy's philandering. It had been fine with Kristin, as it kept Buddy for years oblivious to their dwindling physical relationship.

An annoying thought flew through Kristin's mind. She remembered seeing the reporter with Avery and Hastings Moment as well. Was it possible that the brothers were behind what was happening to her? Hastings was dead, but what about Avery? Was Avery somehow working with this reporter to get back at her?

The reporter had her tapes.

The note left behind clearly spoke of that fact. Kristin knew that Jim was aware of the video, as he in fact had encouraged the idea when Kristin had broached it. But Kristin was pretty sure Jim had no idea where the master files were kept.

When she had left to attend her son's graduation, Kristin had been at a loss as to what to do about her missing files. She was even more perplexed by the thought that the voice had abandoned her, and now seemed to be working with the reporter against her. Kristin knew that the voice had a relationship with the brothers as well. When Hastings had been murdered, the voice had been beside itself with rage, acting as if a best friend had been killed. It kept muttering about how unfair it was that someone else had absorbed what was rightly his. It was one of the few times that Kristin was afraid of the voice. Fortunately, the voice had quickly returned to its normal demeanor, and over the preceding years had been a constant source of good ideas.

Kristin shrugged off the thought, once again returning to Buddy as the most likely source of her problems. It made sense now, why that FBI agent had been dogging her tracks for all these years. What didn't make sense was why they had not arrested her for attempting to kill Buddy. Kristin had a hard time believing what Buddy had told her. He had said that he refused to testify against her, even though he had told the FBI agent exactly what she had done. Instead Buddy had said that what she had done had played a role in "saving" him. He had gone on babbling about the same nonsense her son had spoken about at the graduation.

That thought mingled with her effects of her fourth drink.

"Maam, we have a limit of three drinks per passenger," the flight attendant had said.

Kristin produced her credit card and demanded another one. The flight attendant had returned with both the receipt and the fourth drink. "Maam" made Kristin feel like she was some old lady. Kristin closed her eyes, letting the dizzying effects of the alcohol take hold even as the same flight attendant announced the preparations for takeoff. Her mind though refused to shut down, instead she was reliving the graduation.

How had her son learned about his real father? Certainly, Buddy did not know about that fact. And if they had figured out his parentage, had they also figured out that Susan was not Buddy's either? That thought merged with the call from Avery, in the morning just prior to her departing for the gym and her unexpected diversion to the holding cell and the battle with the FBI and Treasury agents. He was at the airport on the plane.

"Kristin, I am on the plane. Transfer the funds, so I know you are going to keep your word this time," his voice surly like a petulant child.

Kristin hesitated only a moment. Could she really afford to part with that much money? Maybe she should keep the portion that Avery was unaware of. She shook that question away. No, the IRS was too close. Better to be free of them, and of Avery. Avery was going to be in for a real surprise when he saw the real amount of the money being placed under his control. Kristin executed the transfer.

"It's done. Avery, have a nice life, and stay out of mine," she said, disconnecting from him immediately.

Well, what's done is done, she thought. A billion dollars poorer but now with an iron clad alibi. She had been so right, almost clairvoyant. Her arrest less than thirty minutes later, had led to the longest sixteen hours of her life, but she had relished the thought that she had made the right decision.

Kristin remembered her son's hug, greeting her and calming her anger at the way she had been treated by that greeter at the graduation. Forced to wait as if she was just another parent coming to the graduation, and waiting was not something Kristin would ever be used to. Already it was as if she had never been so close to being the wife of the vice president.

That thought started her mind racing down another path. Her husband, the coward and the jerk, had not waited to see Kristin emerge victorious from the confrontation with both the IRS agents and the FBI agent. When she finally caught up with Jim, she was going to give him more than just a piece of her mind. Then she remembered the tape, Jim with that reporter, and her anger deepened. In her mind she saw the woman, riding her husband like he was a prize stallion, and her smile upwards at the camera. Kristin closed her eyes, reliving again that scene.

She felt, more than heard the woman calling her. "Maam, we've landed, you need to get off," the voice said.

She felt her shoulders being rocked, and finally she reopened her eyes. Kristin took in the face the attendant and realized she had fallen asleep. This attendant was not the same one who had brought her the drinks, and in fact, it was obvious that everyone else had already departed from the plane. Kristin tried to stand up and it took a moment for her to realize why she couldn't. Her seat belt was still attached. She unbuckled and finally grabbed her overnight case from the overhead bin and headed for the door. There were already people coming down the ramp, the plane was being reloaded for the next trip. She glanced at her watch, and gasped. They must have been on the ground for thirty minutes before she had finally woken up.

Kristin thought about complaining to the desk agent, but it was clear that unless she wanted to create a scene, she better just keep going. Besides, she now realized she really needed to pee. Kristin dashed into the closest bathroom and was happy to find an open stall. When she was done, she found her way over to the sink and stared at her reflection in the mirror. What she saw, did not fill her with hope. Her eyes were sunken and her normally taut skin on her face seemed suddenly to be filling with wrinkles. She found her sunglasses in her purse and put them on, and then found her hat and covered her head. Staring at the reflection now, she felt somewhat better. At least she would be less recognizable until she had a chance to freshen up.

Maybe Jim would take her to dinner. She could go home, take a quick shower, and freshen up, and then they could go out on the town. Then she remembered again what Jim had done, and the old anger returned. Finally, she turned and headed for the door of the restroom the same moment her phone rang. She fumbled for her phone and looked. It was Earl.

'This is Kristin," she snapped, her old confidence quickly returning to her voice.

"Hi Mrs. Rosewood, it's Earl. I'm in baggage claim. Just making sure you made it, as your bag was the last one at baggage claim. Just want to be sure you were okay, Maam."

There was that word again. 'Maam". It made Kristin feel even older than she was.

"I'm fine. I'll meet you there in a few minutes. I just needed to stop and get something to eat.," she said.

The lie flowed easily off her tongue. Yet, even as she told the lie, her thoughts asked why she needed to lie to Earl. He was just the driver. He didn't need to be given an excuse for her being late. Besides, she paid him well, and if she was late, he could just wait for her to arrive.

The drive back to the suite was uneventful. The suite was as she had left it. Jim was still not home, and two calls to his cell phone resulted in two un-left voice mails. Kristin knew that she could not trust herself to leave a voice message that would do anything but keep Jim away for longer. She wandered around the suite that was now neat and clean. Her maid had done an exceptional job of restoring the order of the living quarters. She spotted the envelope, the large manila type, sitting on the credenza.

The envelope bore the return address of Gregory, Hank, Ipesito LLP, and had clearly arrived by messenger, as no postage or other delivery method was indicated. Kristin had not heard of the legal firm before, but she chose to take the envelope to the living room, figuring it probably would be better to be sitting down before she opened it. There had been just too many surprises in the last two days.

Opening the envelope, she read the enclosed documents quickly, before laying the documents beside her. Jim would not be coming back. The documents announced that he was filing for divorce and made it clear that it would be better that Kristin just accept the situation, after all the evidence of her infidelity was just to abundant. Kristin laid her head back on the couch and kicked off her shoes. Amazingly, no sadness swept over her. Instead her thoughts turned to Jim and to the reporter and the final video left behind as a memorial to their recent activities.

So, Jim wanted out.

Kristin's eyes popped open. The thought literally lit up her face. He wanted out, and she knew exactly what she was going to do about that. Two could play that game. He thought he had her over a barrel, but he was wrong. She stood up from the coach and walked back to her office, fearful that perhaps even this idea might be thwarted. But the file was still there, and the smiling woman's face as she disconnected the camera was still plastered on the screen.

CHAPTER 14 – WELCOME TO BWI

Ken had never been in Thurgood Marshall Airport, before. He had done a short review of the airport online, and discovered it was also known as BWI but had been founded as Friendship airport before it had its name changed. The flight from Grand Rapids was the cheapest flight he could find. Neither Dulles nor National Airport, the two other airports serving the Washington D.C. area, had anything cheaper. The one direct flight to Dulles cost two and a half times as much as the flight to BWI. While it had only cost $300 for the flight to BWI, the flight still would take quite a bite out of their family's weekly finances, especially after having paid for the flight to Tennessee on Saturday to attend Jim Houses' graduation. He'd have to explain to Bernice why he had paid for this flight personally, but the need to confront Kristin with what he knew or suspected made the flight necessary. There just wasn't enough proof yet, to bill the town for this flight to meet with Kristin. Besides, he was now convinced that Kristin's life was also in danger. It was so strange, but he was going to save a murderer from being murdered.

On the other hand, he also wanted the chance to confront Peg Ryan, if possible. He would need to handle that meeting with much more finesse. She was also a public figure like Kristin, and it was obvious that his proof was going to have to be iron clad, in order to get to her.

He had sent all the evidence he had to Larry Smithers at the FBI, the same agent who had been working with Buddy House for all of these years. Ken was hoping that perhaps Larry would be able to tie down the last few facts that would cement the case against Peg. Ken wasn't sure whether Larry would be able to pull any strings and get the warrant to search Peg Ryan's home in D.C.. But Ken was confident, that if they did get inside her house, the final proof would be found. He believed with all the intuition he had, that the trophies of the murder would be found there.

He had been encouraged to go both by his father and by Glenn to meet Kristin. The results of his planned dinner with his father had turned out as a bit of a surprise. Ken had arrived at this father's house right at 8:30 PM, but when his father had opened the door, Ken saw the table set, with food already steaming waiting for his arrival. Ken had wanted to take his father out, so that neither Buddy nor Glenn would over hear their conversation, but it was obvious that his father had other plans.

"Hi, son," his father's greeting shortened as he took in Ken's obvious discomfort.

Ken saw his father's eyes, and he knew that his father had already seen his apprehension as he spied the set table.

"Buddy's not here, he's over at Jim and Susan's grandparents' home, talking with Kristin's parents," his father said, removing one of Ken's concerns.

But Glenn stood in the kitchen, looking in Ken's direction. "I think Glenn may be able to help you, Ken. I asked him to stay, as I assume this is about Hasting's death, and you have figured out something you want to share with me, to get my reaction?" the statement coming out as the question but Ken knew it was not a question, but an assertion . Ken looked at Glenn again, and then nodded at his father. As normal, his father was already further ahead in figuring out Ken's purpose, and he accepted his father's decision to include Glenn.

Ken slipped by his father and entered the house.

The flight had left on Monday morning, and now Ken stood staring at the five-foot stained glass crab that decorated the arrival lobby at the airport. People swept around him, and he pondered what he should do. He was sure he looked odd, standing in his dress uniform considering the crab, while he pondered his next move. The Grand Rapids' airport felt small compared to this airport, and Ken was painfully aware that he was a small town sheriff in a really big town place. There were probably more people in this airport right now, than lived in his town. Ken watched the crowd of people walking past him and looked over the banister at the hundreds of people standing in lines to get tickets, and revised his estimate. There were more people here than in the entire county his town was a part of.

He wondered how Kristin and Peg had made the transition from their small-town roots to this new metropolitan existence, and what had caused them to leave such a trail of destruction in the much more placid environment that they had grown up in. Certainly, the crimes committed belonged more to the big city setting, or at least that is what he had told himself. One of Glenn's comments from the other evening though had caused him to rethink that feeling.

"Evil doesn't respect geography or culture. Murder by humans first came into existence just after the fall. Cain's murder of Abel, occurred in a truly rural setting. There were only a few people alive, yet the number of people, did not matter. Cain was a farmer, Abel was a farmer. One brought an offering from the ground, the other an offering from the flock. Both were in a farming community led by their parents. They both tended the earth and cared for animals. If murder could touch them, why do you think it so odd, that murder would not touch our town? I've always found it interesting that Cain's offering was not accepted by God. Was it that Cain's offering should have been from the flock and not the ground, or was it something else, something within Cain that made the offering unacceptable. I believe the same thing that made his offering unacceptable also made the first murder possible. Living inside each of us is the root of evil, without God's grace and his protection, that root can quickly sprout. The Lord told Cain that, but he did not listen and in short order, Abel was dead.

Our Lord called Satan both a murderer and a liar. Who do you think Satan murdered?

Remember, before he tempted Eve and through her Adam, there was no death. So, the first real murderer is Satan, and Satan has not changed. He still wants to nurse that evil root until every man becomes a murderer like he is. And from what you have said, both Peg and Kristin have been fooling around with and listening to forces who have been busily fertilizing that root of evil. No, what you have seen is not strange at all."

That brief exchange had come when Ken had commented on the strangeness of having Hastings murder occur in such a small town, and now that Ken was convinced that another murder had long been hidden but was about to come to light, making the town victim to two such events was even more bizarre.. Glenn's statement had given Ken much to think about. Glenn had also warned him that confronting both women was going to bring him face to face with the evil behind the events, but at the same time he had encouraged him to go, with the hope that one or both might still be rescued from the destruction that lay immediately before them.

Being the son of a pastor, Ken had heard this before, but coming from Glenn, the words seemed to have even more force. Ken knew that while his father had confronted many different evils, Glenn had experienced even more than his father had. There was a sense of urgency in Glenn's thoughts and words, that in the end convinced Ken to make the trip.

He had tried to reach both Kristin and Peg on Sunday, thinking it better that he get an appointment, but in both cases only voice mails had greeted him, and he had decided against leaving messages. He needed to hear their voices, to gauge the impact of his words on them. He left no message, as he did not want to prepare them more than he had to, for his arrival. He decided against trying to reach them again, until he was in the area. Now that he was here he wondered at the wisdom of not having gotten an appointment, but it was too late to turn back.

Ken had Kristin's address, and he also had the address of the news station that Peg Ryan worked for. Ken looked around, saw the signs pointing for baggage claim, rental cars, and restaurants, and headed towards the restaurants. He found the Phillips Crab's restaurant, and discovered that it was already crowded, but he was seated immediately and gratefully in a corner. He ordered his early lunch and while he waited, he dialed the news channel first.

"KTVW channel 4 on your side, how can I help you?" the receptionist voice chipper and inviting, with a bit of the nasally clip that hinted at the woman's nationality.

"Hi, I am Sheriff Ken Farr from Hitchenburgh Michigan, and I would like to speak with Peg Ryan please," Ken said.

'You and everyone else," the voice said, seemingly amused at another caller asking for Peg.

"Peg's on assignment, Sheriff and we are not expecting her back until late this evening, and I should tell you, she has a list a mile long of people who want to speak with her. She's become something of a sensation, since she broke the twin stories, and all the major news stations are trying to interview her for their own shows as well," she added with a tinge of pride in her voice.

"You'll have to get in line, unless she's expecting your call, or you have something to add to her stories," the woman laughed and then waited for his response.

"Yes, I am sure that the arrest of Kristin Rosewood and the demise of her husband's running for the VP spot, has a lot of people talking," Ken said, but before he could add any more, the receptionist laughed.

"Honey, that's old news. Haven't you heard! The big news today is the Fed's arrested the man who was in cahoots with Kristin Rosewood, and he is spilling his guts about the truth on Kristin's actual financial chicanery, and Jim Rosewood, well he has filed for divorce from his wife and Peg broke that news as well. Turns out Ms. Rosewood is our very own madam butterfly and the list of who she has been sleeping with is the who's who in D.C. Yep, everyone is talking about Peg Ryan, and her stories. It's rocking the city!" she added.

It sounded like the news channel was covering stories normally resigned to the gossip magazines of the supermarket checkout lines, but Ken knew that in D.C., this probably really was big news.

"I am here on official business, and I really do need to speak with her. How do I get a hold of her?" Ken asked.

"Official business?" the voice at the end of the line chuckled again, and then turned serious.

"Sheriff, I have had calls from the Secretary of the Treasury, someone claiming to be the White House operator calling for the Vice President, and several other folks claiming "official business", so as I said, you'll have to get in line and somehow, I suspect that they will be in line in front of you."

The last statement felt a little like Ken was being relegated to the position of a commoner amongst the royalty. That inference and the obvious disdain in the woman's voice, brought Ken's blood to a near boil.

"Do you have a message for Ms. Ryan? I'll deliver it, but can't promise you will get a call back," she said.

Ken thought about that for a moment, pressing down on his anger that had suddenly appeared. He wanted to say, "Yes, please tell Ms. Ryan it's about her murdering Hastings Moment," but he knew he still did not have enough to make that charge stick. Besides he knew that if he had enough evidence, he would not be looking for an audience with the in-demand reporter.

"Yes, please tell Ms. Ryan that I understand she's not even in the top ten, and I believe she ranked out somewhere in the top twenty and tell her I found both messages she left. Also, please tell her thanks for the tip and that I would like to know how she knew about the plane and I need her to return the evidence she took," Ken said.

Ken knew that he was exposing about half of what he had figured out, but he also knew his only chance of getting the reporter's attention was threatening her with what he had learned.

The receptionist repeated back the strange message, her lack of surprise telling Ken that apparently many such bizarre messages arrived regularly. Ken left his cell phone number, and made the receptionist repeat it back, just to be sure. Just before he disconnected, he added, "Listen, please also tell Peg, that the forces she is in partnership with, only want her destruction, and I'm trying to prevent that."

After he disconnected, he thought through the impromptu message. He was still wondering about it when his lunch order arrived. He barely tasted the crab cake he had ordered, even though he had heard that crab cakes were a Maryland specialty. He dialed Kristin's number between bites and was surprised when the phone was answered.

"Kristin Rosewood's office," the woman's voice said.

"Hi, I am Sheriff Ken Farr from Hitchenburgh Michigan, and I would like to speak with Kristin please," Ken said.

"I'm sorry but Ms. Rosewood is not available, would you like to leave a message? she answered.

Once again, Ken felt his anger pushing him to shout at the woman. Instead he said, "Would you tell Kristin that I know about Avery and Hastings, and I know what she did to Craig Housher."

Ken took a gamble and added, "I'll hold, deliver that message, and if she still doesn't want to talk to me, then I will leave my phone number."

The woman said nothing, and the click on the phone left Ken wondering whether he had been disconnected. But the phone still showed that he was connected to the number, although only silence reigned.

Ken thought about his last comment, the one about Craig Houser. He had spent the better part of the last week putting together everything he could about Craig's apparent suicide. The file on the event was sketchy at best. Ken's predecessor as Sheriff, Devin Little, had been meticulous, yet this case file had minimum notes. Nothing that showed that Kristin had been pregnant with her son Jim at the time of the suicide. Not until Jenny Housher had broken down at his father's house, and later showed him the photo of Craig, which was a dead give away from the true parentage of Jim, had anyone questioned whether Buddy House was really Jim's father.

Now that it was obvious that Buddy was not Jim's father and that Craig instead was, things started falling into place. The realization that Avery Moment must be Susan's father, moved things along even further.

Everything Ken had learned about Craig, made the suicide more nonsensical. Craig by all accounts was a strong and committed Christian, someone even Glenn had vouched for. Also, despite Jenny's questioning of just how much Craig really had loved her and their son, everything Ken had been able to learn pointed to that very fact. There was no doubt that Craig had fallen for Kristin, but there was too much evidence that pointed to the unlikelihood of Craig opting for suicide as an escape. Everything Ken had learned about the man, seemed to point to the fact that he would have owned his sin, and tried to make things right. But if it wasn't suicide that left only one thing. Someone had killed Craig and made it look like suicide.

The only person Ken could see with a motive for that, was Kristin. Ken had built a time line, and it was obvious that the suicide tied closely to the exposures of several people who had relationships with Kristin. Buddy had willingly helped Ken with the time line, not knowing that Ken was beginning to suspect that Craig's death wasn't a suicide and that Kristin was the likely suspect. His wedding to Kristin conveniently hid the pregnancy from the world, but Buddy had admitted that he had known Kristin was pregnant, and he had assumed that he was the father.

Now even Buddy understood that he had been duped, but still appeared oblivious to the answer of the question of why Kristin choose to mislead Buddy as well. Buddy had described his use of Kristin's black book, with the entries chronicling all of Kristin's liaisons with different influential people in Hitchenburgh. Buddy freely admitted the extorting of money from most of the individuals after making a demonstration of the two teachers, to get the rest of the individuals to pay up. Craig's suicide seemed to play right into those plans, as it communicated the desperateness and hopelessness of trying to fight Buddy's accusations, or Kristin's potential proof. In the end, the money had started Buddy on his way to building his empire, and gave Kristin what she desired the most as well. Money was the key to power and influence. Neither Buddy nor Kristin had ever looked back or questioned what they were doing.

It was Buddy's description of Kristin's shooting him, and the apparent ease with which she did it, that cemented for Ken, Kristin's role in Craig's death. The first murder was always way more difficult that the future ones. Ken had been left wondering if there were even more murders in her past before she had tried to kill Buddy, or if Buddy really was just her second one. The phone suddenly clicked back on, and a different woman's voice brought Ken's focus back to the present.

"This is Kristin Rosewood, how can I help you Sheriff Farr?," Kristin said.

Ken decided it was better to handle the conversation with the same formality that Kristin's question had set in place.

"Ms. Rosewood, I am here in the D.C. area, and I believe it would be better that I meet with you face to face to discuss that. When can we meet?" Ken stated flatly.

Kristin didn't miss a beat, seemingly unsurprised that Ken was already in the area.

"I've got a 5:00 PM dinner engagement, so I will be leaving at 4:00 PM, I can meet you at our residence at 3:00 PM, you know where I live?" Kristin asked.

Ken repeated the address he had memorized, and Kristin confirmed his information was correct.

"I look forward to our discussion sheriff, I am sure it will be interesting," Kristin said, and the line clicked off.

Ken glanced at his phone, and the time display. It was 12:45 PM and suddenly the only thing Ken could think about was getting to Kristin's home. He suspected that he could find it easy enough, but he still had to rent the car, and then make the hour drive to Arlington from the airport. He looked at the half-eaten crab cake, not even remembering eating as much as the plate indicated. He looked at the check, dropped a twenty on the table and left.

CHAPTER 15 – EXPOSED

Kristin looked at the phone. The call from Ken Farr fit right in to the misery that her life had become over the last forty-eight hours. She had started planning her counter attack to her husband's defection from both their marriage and from the events they had orchestrated together. Kristin knew that Peg Ryan was going to be a formidable opponent, but she was beginning to suspect that she may have misjudged just how formidable.

Kristin made the copies of the video that demonstrated both Peg's participation in the very practices being used against Kristin and showed her wayward husband at his worst. She called a number of contacts in the media, whose names had not yet been linked to her activities, and used the threat of that added exposure to get them to at least look at her new evidence. What she had not counted on, was the speed at which those facts had gotten back to Peg. Apparently Peg also had pull with the three men Kristin had approached, and all three had declined doing anything with the new information. It was the third man, who had given up the fact that the only thing he feared more than Kristin's exposure was the exposure Peg Ryan could and would do to him.

Then came the news on Sunday morning of the arrest of Avery Moment. As it turned out he had not left the US, but instead had flown back to Florida, and headed back to the home he owned in Vero Beach, Florida. Apparently, the documents that Kristin had so skillfully used to point the finger at Avery, became the basis of the arrest warrants put out for Avery. Kristin had turned on the television on Sunday morning to catch some of the Washington Political talk shows, to hear whether she was still in the news, only to catch the special bulletin carried on KTVW channel 4 where Peg Ryan stood just outside a small terminal with the sign 'Vero Beach Municipal Airport" just to the left of her. Kristin missed the opening scene, catching Peg after the introduction.

"KTVW Channel 4 learned late yesterday of the arrest warrant for Avery Moment, the investor implicated in the tax avoidance scheme of Kristin Rosewood, the wife of the former vice presidential candidate Senator Jim Rosewood. We learned as well that the FBI and Treasury Agents had tracked Mr. Moment through airline reservations, flying from the Washington D.C. area, to New York, where he had apparently bought tickets for Columbia South America. However, for some reason Mr. Moment did not fly to Columbia, a country with no extradition agreement with the US. Instead he boarded a chartered jet that flew him back to Vero Beach Florida, where we are told he owns a home on the beach here. This was the scene, just moments ago here in Florida.

The scene changed, obviously a taping of the earlier events. Kristin watched as three men surrounding Avery marched him out of the terminal. The background was dim, so it was obviously early in the morning. Peg's back and then face came into view, as the camera man jockeyed the camera to get a better picture of everything that was going on.

'Mr. Moment, can you comment on the charges against you? How are you involved with Kristin Rosewood?" Peg's questions coming out without any break to allow a response. At the mention of Kristin's name, Avery stopped dead in his tracks, causing one of the men escorting him to nearly trip. Avery then yelled at the top of his lungs,

"That bitch set me up. She's the one they should be arresting not me!", he yelled.

The three men began to man handle Avery, pushing him towards the waiting car. Avery struggled against the men, continuing to yell, much of it unintelligible. Then suddenly his words took on clarity as the men forced him into the back seat of the car. Just before the car door slammed shut, Avery shouted:

'Kristin, I am going to get you for this. You hear me, you're going to pay!"

The scene returned to the present with Peg continuing her commentary.

"As you can see, Mr. Moment obviously is upset and apparently believes that Ms. Rosewood had set him up for the arrest that you just saw occur. We have learned from our sources, that Mr. Moment recently came into the possession of over a billion dollars of ill-gotten gain, which is the focus of the recent investigation into Ms. Rosewood's activities. Despite the apology given by the head of the financial fraud division of the IRS, apparently Ms. Rosewood is far from being in the clear. We will keep you informed of events as they move forward. This is Peg Ryan reporting from Vero Beach, Florida for KTVW Channel Four."

Kristin was stunned, she flipped the channel, not waiting to hear anymore commentary, but on the next channel, there was Peg Ryan's face again, this time being interviewed by another channel's news anchor. The same tape of Avery's arrest was playing, and Peg answered other questions posed by that anchor. Kristin listened for a few minutes, and then flipped the channel again, and there she was again.

"How in the world, had she pulled that one off," Kristin asked herself.

It was as if she had single handedly become the most important person in the world for that Sunday morning. Kristin decided she might as well watch the shows, to see what other damage Peg would do. In every show Peg would drop a few more delectable supposed facts.

It wasn't until the third show, fully two hours after Kristin had seen the first report, that Peg dropped the second bomb shell announcement. The news anchor had just asked Peg whether she had spoken to Senator Jim Rosen about the charges being made by Avery, when Peg announced for the whole world, what Kristin had learned only two nights before.

"Well, yes I have spoken to Senator Rosewood, and as you can imagine, he is very disturbed by all of the controversy surrounding his wife, but he has decided not to comment on his wife's situation until their divorce is final." Peg stated.

"Divorce?", the news anchor said, disbelief and surprise sharing equal shares as the anchor grasped the significance of what Peg had just said.

"Yes, that is right, Senator Rosewood filed for divorce from his wife two days ago," Peg said, again acting like this news was no news at all.

Kristin just stared. So now the whole world knew. She wasn't surprised that the divorce was becoming public, just the manner that it did was a surprise. The next ten minutes was painful but amusing to watch. Peg continued to act like this news was no news at all, while feeding the anchor just a little more fact after each question. Most of what she said, was accurate, but some of it was clearly guesses, although very good guesses. But she had quoted almost directly from the divorce papers the reason for Jim Rosewoods request for divorce. Peg called it "marital infidelity" but then added a quip about how many men in Washington had their names in Kristin's little black book. And then she let slip seemingly by accident, that there were also more than one hundred hours of video documenting many of those illicit meetings.

"It sounds like you have seen those videos?" the anchor asked.

Peg smiled and answered,

"Yes, of course, my sources gave them to me, and I gave them to the Senator." The anchor went apoplectic. Kristin saw the face of the anchor, who was suddenly silent, as if not knowing what to ask next. Kristin knew that the face of the anchor was all too clearly visible on one of the missing videos.

Kristin's private phone rang. It was her secretary.

"Mrs. Rosewood, the phone is ringing off the hook! I am getting hundreds of calls from news channels, looking for you to comment on some story that Peg Ryan broke about you. What do you want me to say?" the harried women asked.

"Janet, pull the plug on the phone and go home. It will all blow over by tomorrow. Just take the day off," Kristin said, knowing that it would likely not be over by the next day.

"Okay Mrs. Rosewood, and oh, a General McIntyre called for you as well. He left a message about getting together for dinner. Said you had mentioned the possibility when you met him at the White House party a week ago. I told him I would give you the message," and then she gave Kristin a phone number and she was gone.

A week ago? More like a lifetime ago, so much had happened in the intervening time.

By two o'clock on Sunday, Kristin had enough. She turned off the television, called Earl, and told him he wasn't going to be needed for the rest of the day, giving him, like Janet, the rest of the day off. She retreated to the bathroom and the soaking tub, and spent the next two hours soaking, and alternating between fuming, thinking and planning. She had expected a rap on the door, and the federal agents waiting to whisk her way again, for another prolonged interview or even arrest. But no knock had come.

At five o'clock she had watched the early news, and on the five channels she had flipped through either Avery or she were still the lead story. Fortunately, by five o'clock, Peg was no longer the lead except on KWTV 4 and Peg had no new revelations during her brief stint in front of the camera. At seven she had finally called General McIntyre.

"This is Tony," the voice said, answering on the third ring.

Kristin was taken aback by his informality, but then realized that she had no idea where the phone number connected her too.

"General McIntyre, its Kristin Rosewood, my secretary gave me a message saying you had called. I'm just calling you back," she said.

"Kristin, thanks for calling me back, I hadn't expected it, based on everything you must be going through right now, how are you?"

Kristin was again almost speechless. His question had the ring of genuine concern, and his voice was neither accusatory nor judging.

"Well General,..

'Kristin, please call me Tony, you can call me General in public, but I'm not calling you as General McIntyre, I am just calling you as myself, and my friends call me Tony," he said.

Once again, Kristin was taken back.

"Okay Tony, frankly I have had better weeks. Not every week that your private life is so completely eviscerated without anyone even asking you about it," she said.

'Tony, I have to ask, why did you call me?" Kristin asked

"Didn't your secretary tell you? I called to see if you would like to do dinner, you mentioned the possibility a week ago, and I was just following up," he said.

Again, the quality of his voice was unlike anything Kristin had expected to hear. He was neither judging or looking for an advantage. She couldn't imagine why he would want to go out with her, especially with everything he must be learning about her.

"Tony, why would you want to go out with me? Right now, anyone that would be seen with me, would be painted with a pretty wide brush, and even you must have concerns," Kristin responded.

'Well Kristin, I thought you might need someone to talk through some of what you are facing, and quite frankly, I was taken by the way you handled yourself at the White House. I can't imagine what you must be dealing with. Anyway, that is why I called, to see if I could help in some way."

Again, if the offer had come from anyone else, or if his tone had been different, she would have known what to say, but his offer seemed to be more than genuine. There was nothing in his voice, or his choice of words, that portrayed anything but real concern, and the desire to help.

"You said dinner, Tony, what did you have in mind?" she asked.

"How about tomorrow evening, say around six. We could meet somewhere, or I can swing by and pick you up, if you prefer," he said.

"You sure you want to be seen with me," Kristin asked again.

He laughed.

"I don't really care what people think. In the end, we are all lonely, and we need friends, regardless of what the world thinks," he said.

"If you don't mind picking me up, I think that will be good, but, let's meet at Bobby's on 9th Avenue, and we can go from there. I think I can slip out without my personal parade of reporters seeing me, and I'll have my chauffeur create a diversion by driving my car right up front, as if I am going somewhere, while I sneak out the back. Would that be okay?" Kristin asked.

"Bobby's on 9th Avenue at 6:00 it is. I'll be the really tall bald guy driving a fairly pedestrian Chevy," he quipped.

Kristin laughed for what felt like the first time, in a long long time.

"General, I remember what you look like," Kristin said.

"It's Tony and I will see you then," and he had hung up.

Kristin stared at the phone. It had been ages since she had talked to any man, who she had not been trying to manipulate, or who had not been trying to manipulate her. She would get to see if her first impression about General Tony McIntyre was correct, that he really was not like most men.

Kristin played the conversation with the General over again in her mind. She could not escape the sense that there was much more to the man. She allowed herself to walk through that day of triumph again, when she was escorted by the General through the White House experience. She had blocked out that experience, as all it did was to serve as a backdrop against which her current situation showed her just how far she had fallen.

It was an irony, that just when she thought she had arrived at the place she had always dreamed of, it was taken away. Not only was the dream removed, but the years of work to get there were now coming back to serve as permanent impediments to ever returning to that dream.

The General's voice had a quality in it she had experienced only a few times before. With a shudder she recalled who the General's tone had reminder her. She opened that mental door as well, one that she had steadfastly refused to open for years. In her mind she heard Craig's gentle voice and marveled at his genuine interest in her. She had been unable to comprehend it twenty-five years ago. But know she remembered and finally understood. He truly had really liked her and wanted what was best for her.

The very thing that had tormented him at the end, was his gentle spirit that had so attracted her. He cared for people deeply. He had cared for her. He had spoken to her of his faith, and she had pushed those words aside, instead desiring what she thought would bring her satisfaction.

She had assumed that what she wanted would also be what he wanted most of all. She never considered the possibility, that the very thing she wanted most, would be his undoing. In the end, she had experienced what at the time was the zenith of what she thought love was. Instead the experience had destroyed the very one she had idolized. He had tried to explain to her why he was devastated by the fact that he had given in to what she had dreamt about since she had first met him. She remembered his words, as if they were spoken yesterday, those words of sorrow, as he tried to explain it to her.

She returned to the present. Refusing to continue thinking about all she had done.

Was it possible that Tony McIntyre like Craig Houser was a Christian? That this fact was why the General's gentle words so reminded her of Craig? She thought through their time together at the White House party, and she recognized his polite deference to her. Here he was, the Joint Chiefs chairman, and she was little more than a want to be politicians' wife, and he had deferred to her. She realized now, that he had never looked on her with the obvious lust of so many of the other men, as had the presidents of both the US and Russia. He also had never leveled a single moment of disdain towards her activities either, as so many of the women at the party had.

Instead he had said that he had been impressed by her at the party.

Looking back, she tried to think through what he might have been impressed about. The only time she had caught him looking at her funny was after the Russian translator had spoken to her about her paper. She remembered seeing the General talking with the translator later, and when done he had looked over at her, while she was busy speaking with a group of Senators that had gravitated towards her, after it was apparent she was now in the inner circle of power.

She remembered glancing up at him, and caught him looking at her, with what... at the time she had dismissed it. But now she remembered, he was looking at her with a look of admiration. Not the type of admiration she would have expected from a man, but a type that spoke about his judgment of her as an equal, something more than just a pretty body and a pretty face.

The knock on the door startled her out of her analysis of Tony. No one was supposed to be allowed up to her suite without a call from the front desk. She slipped into the foyer and flipped on the security camera that revealed who was waiting in the lobby outside her door. She recognized the man, his face clearly looking at the camera as if he knew she was staring right back at him. She looked around the lobby, searching for other unannounced guests. The man backed up from the camera, again as if he knew that she needed the broader view to confirm that only he was waiting for her. He appeared to be alone. She watched the man as he folded his hands resting them on the top of the staff he carried with him.

Again, he stared into the camera, seemingly knowing that she was right there examining him. Kristin hesitated and then finally decided not to use the speaker system. She steeled herself, checking herself in the mirror that hung beside the door, she tucked a loose strand of her hair, back behind her ear, and then she opened the door.

CHAPTER 16 – DISCOVERY

By the time sheriff Ken Farr called the next morning, Kristin had dodged more than twenty different calls from news organizations seeking her to comment on everything that Peg Ryan had exposed. Despite the nagging fear that at any moment the next knock on the door would be either the FBI or the IRS agents, looking to arrest her again. Her nighttime visitor had told her that they would eventually figure it all out, but by then, it would be too late. That had brought her a momentary relief, but then he had gone on, telling her that the real danger confronting her did not come from either agency.

She had told herself that this was likely only because neither agency would want to go through the embarrassment of re-arresting her, only to discover that they had missed something that would cause them to have to issue another apology. No, this time they were waiting until they were confident that every I was dotted, and every T crossed.

Before he had left, he had handed her a small book, opening to a part that was marked. She had read the portion, and he had explained it to her. His words would have sounded like nonsense to her just a few weeks ago, but now they made perfect sense. Once again, Craig's voice echoed in her mind as he spoke, and her visitor's warning rang with the surety that turned her blood cold. Kristin remembered Craig's light touch on her forehead some twenty-five years ago, as he had urged her to turn her mind on considering what he had said. His finger touching the spot right above her nose, the first time he had ever touched her.

"Use what you have been given Kristin, turn that amazing mind to focus on the truth, and it will set you free," his words still sending shivers up her back. Back then, it was that light touch on her forehead that added to the sensation, but now the touch was a memory, and his words held even a greater power. How had she been so blind she asked herself, and then the crushing weight of what she had done returned.

She looked at the visitor and broke down, weeping unhindered as the full weight of her life flooded over her. She felt his gentle embrace, supporting her shaking frame.

He had stayed under a half hour.

The sheriff's call, and his altogether straight forward accusation that she had hidden the identity of her children's fathers, and the fact that he had correctly identified not only Craig Houser as Jim's father, but also Avery Moment as Susan's, had shaken her. But it was his final assertion, that he knew what she had done to Craig, that had brought her to her knees. Finally, the door that had been opened a crack in her dream, and then further by Tony's voice, and finally by the visitor, flew open. She relived Craig's death, and her role in it.

Where had she gone wrong? At first the question appeared to be, what evidence had she left that would lead Sheriff Farr to the conclusion that she had killed Craig, but it quickly morphed into her examining the why she did what she had. Craig's words mixed with the visitors' words. By the time the lobby attendant called up to her, to let her know that a Sheriff Ken Farr was in the lobby to see her, she had answered the question that mattered most.

"Please send him up, I'll meet him at the elevator upstairs," Kristin told the attendant.

She had dressed to head out to meet Tony. She had not thought about the fact that the Sheriff would see her like this. But at this point, it really didn't matter. She would have to get through this painful interview, and then hopefully escape to meet Tony and to see if perhaps, he had any insight into what she could do, to save herself from what she had done and to escape the judgment she saw looming over her.

Picking something that was loose enough to hide what she had chosen to wear underneath was difficult. She had almost thrown it out, this surprise gift from her supposedly dead but obviously completely alive former husband, but her visitor had reinforced Buddy's warning. He knew something was about to happen, and for once she had accepted that there were forces far greater than what she controlled at play here. His warning and brief discussion about her former "voice" had caused her to finally admit something she had refused to think about. The voice was more than just her own internal personality talking. The voice's departure had ensured that she realized that fact. Her internal floors were swept clean, and her visitor warned what would happen if the voice returned before she had filled that vacant space. She was still pondering that warning, wondering what she could fill it with. The visitor had not spoken about that.

The light blue dress with the loose bodice and the equally sculpted side panels allowed her to wear the gift, without it being ready observable. Amazingly, after she was fully dressed, she hardly noticed that she had it on.

For Ken, the drive from BWI to Kristin's home in Arlington was uneventful. During the drive he had thought through what he was going to say to Kristin. Both his father and Glenn had cautioned Ken, that Kristin had been fooling herself about the helpful nature of the forces in league with her.

"Remember, they are looking to destroy her, and if they understand you as a threat to that plan, they will attack you as well. Pray for her, but pray for yourself, that you might be prepared for that attack," his father had warned.

It always amazed Ken, that his father always saw everything in this life with a spiritual dimension. Ken was interested in solving a murder, and in the process, he had uncovered another murder hidden for years, but his father seemed unconcerned about solving these and remained unsurprised by the facts Ken now believed. Instead his father was sure that forces beyond the people's own nature were at work, and present in everything that was occurring. Glenn shared his father's conviction.

Ken had taken the time during the drive down the Baltimore- Washington Parkway, and then onto Route 395 heading towards Arlington, not only thinking through what he was going to say to Kristin, but also praying for his own strength, and praying that perhaps Kristin would react differently to his accusations than he expected. He also prayed that he not meet any of the forces his father and Glenn had warned him of.

Meeting the two angels that seemed to accompany Glenn so often, had been unnerving enough. He had seen their power only once, and the destruction of the Parlor in Hitchenburgh, and the forty lives that were snuffed out at the same time, still left him feeling shaken. And those angels were "good" angels. Try as he may, he still had questions about how they could be good and participate in the destruction he had seen. His father had explained it, and Ken understood it intellectually, but that didn't change the strange queasiness he felt every time he considered the events. Meeting other angels using their power for evil purposes was not something Ken had any desire to face.

Ken found Kristin's building, but he had to park almost two blocks away, and then walk to the building. The desk attendant had been polite, and had called Kristin immediately, announcing his arrival. She nodded as she listened to Kristin's response to her call.

"Sheriff take the elevator on the right to the sixth floor. Ms. Rosewood said she would meet you in the elevator lobby. Her suite is the only one on that floor, but she said she would be waiting for you," the attendant said.

Ken marveled at the gleaming aluminum elevator, big enough to hold at least ten people, yet designed to service a building probably with under twenty residences. An attendant, a door man, and probably security people as well, and this for maybe thirty people. Ken marveled again at what real wealth could afford. He spent the last few seconds, with his eyes closed, praying another quick prayer.

The elevator chimed, indicating it had arrived at its destination, and Ken opened his eyes and watched as the door opened. He stepped into the foyer, and saw a woman seated on the bench just outside the elevator door against a window that delivered a floor to ceiling view of the city just west of the building. Behind him, he sensed the mirror window, that must be delivering the panoramic view of what lie east of the building. The windows appeared to have some coating, as the light coming in had a muted tone, cutting out the brightness of the sun.

Against the filtered light coming from the window, the woman's figure was undeniably striking. Her blond shoulder length hair framed her face, and her greenish blue eyes, emanated intelligence. Each of her facial features, from her perfectly framed and shaped nose, to the full and sensuous lips accented her beauty.

She stood, walking quickly towards him. Ken took it all in. He instantly understood how Kristin had impacted so many people. She was stunning.

It was also then that Ken realized that unlike all the revealing or skin-tight fashions he had seen her in, today she was wearing a simple dress, almost similar to what his own wife Beatrice would wear.

"Sheriff Farr, I would say it is a pleasure to meet you, but then you would know that was a lie," Kristin said.

Kristin stood about three feet from Ken, and did not offer her hand in greeting, or make any other kind of greeting gesture. Her words had been delivered neither with a tone of anger, or a tone of fear, simply conveying the facts of the situation, with an air of resignation that this interview needed to take place.

"This way please," she said turning towards an open door, which led into the residence. Ken followed, praying silently to himself that he be able to say what he had come to say, and get out of here in one piece. Suddenly the wisdom of meeting this woman here, by himself, left him questioning his judgment. Surely it would have been better to have another person with him, he reasoned. At that very moment, the elevator chimed again, and Ken stopped turning just as he saw Kristin stopping to turn as well, to see who else might be arriving. Ken could see in Kristin's surprised look, the questioning accusation that she believed Ken had come with someone else. Ken shook his head, telling her without words, that whoever was arriving was not by his invitation.

To Ken's astonishment a woman stepped from the car. There was no mistaking who it was, the crooked seeming damaged smile that spread across her face instantly reminding Ken of his several meetings with the woman in the past. Ken saw her expression turn into a cross between a sneer and a toothy grin as she took in the look of surprise Ken was sure was registering on his face. Ignoring Ken, she said to Kristin,

"Well Kristin, I thought it was probably time for us to meet you, to be more formally introduced," she said.

The woman slipped by the stunned Ken, standing about six feet away from Kristin. She raised one of her hands, the other still nestled against her body, as if hiding something.

'I'm Peg Ryan," the woman said.

Ken saw the emotion race through Kristin's face and then suddenly disappear, and her eyes flashed from the resignation Ken had seen in them just seconds ago, to a cold fury.

"I know who you are, what are you doing here?" Kristin's response; not moving to shake the woman's hand or draw any closer.

"As I said, I thought it was time for us to formally meet, and we wanted to be here to make sure you didn't do anything stupid, like really tell the sheriff here what you have been thinking about, or going to meet anyone who might fill your head with similar nonsense," the woman said.

Ken noted the strange plurals the woman was using in her speech.

He also saw that Kristin was staring at the woman with laser intensity while her face revealed nothing of what she was thinking.

"Ms. Ryan as you know I have left you several messages as well, and I have some questions for you as well," Ken said, trying to break into the stare down that was going on between the two women.

The woman turned just slightly looking at Ken, and then turning back to Kristin, even as she said:

"We know who you are sheriff, and until you have a warrant or someone with you with authority I advise you to stay silent and stay out of this discussion. It doesn't pertain to you," the woman said.

But the voice was different, it was no longer the melodic woman's voice, but a deeper gravelly voice.

Ken saw the menace in the woman's face, and for the first time saw a different emotion, and apparent recognition sweeping across Kristin's face, replaced quickly by a look of fear.

"That's right dearie, I'm with Peg now. She's mine, just as you are mine, and I will not allow you to think you can escape. You have had the benefits from what I gave you and now you think I will let you escape without giving me what you owe?"

The voice was both taunting and pushing at the same time and Peg was moving closer to Kristin. Ken found himself walking towards the woman, and then past her, stepping between her and Kristin when little more than three feet separated them. Ken stared into the eyes of Peg Ryan.

"I think I know what you are. I also suspect that you know that I am close to proving that Ms. Ryan murdered Hastings Moment. I am sure that you played a role in that as well, as I suspect that Hastings was a pawn you decided to discard," Ken said.

"Step aside Sheriff, you do not belong here, and there is nothing you can say or do that will come between me and what belongs to me," the voice said.

Ken took in the woman's gleaming eyes and he saw at that instant many eyes seemingly floating within the woman's eyes.

Ken remembered a story that Glenn had shared, and he remembered his Father's own sermon, and he knew both the lie the voice had spoken as well as a certainty as to what he was now face to face with.

"The Lord rebuke you," Ken said, quietly, but looking straight into the woman's eyes. The words seemingly to come from some secret door that had suddenly sprung open in Ken's mind.

Emotions rippled through the woman's face.

"The Lord rebuke you," Ken repeated this time more forcefully and this time stepping towards the woman.

Ken saw the woman's hand flashing towards him, and it was the first time he recognized the object her hand was holding. Ken's reflexes took over, blocking the surprising quick slicing move, feeling the woman's arm hitting his blocking arm, he grabbed her wrist with his other hand flipping her hand to the side, hearing the distinct snapping of bones, as the knife she had been hiding suddenly fell to the floor from the disabled hand.

The woman let out a cry, much lower in volume than what Ken had expected, just as Kristin rushed by both of them, and jumped into the elevator that still waited open having just delivered Peg.

"Wait, Kristin, no, don't go," the voice now pleading, all sense of triumph removed.

But the door closed, and Kristin was gone.

Peg Ryan, however, wasn't done and despite her broken wrist, she struck out at Ken with her good hand that turned into a fist at the last moment, a strange backwards movement that Ken had not expected. The blow connected with his cheek just below his eye, and Ken was amazed at the strength in that punch, which sent him reeling sideways and falling to the floor. At the same moment, the other elevator pinged open, and out stepped four men. Ken recognized two of the men immediately, but two others he did not recognized were dressed in police uniforms. Seeing Ken sprawled on the floor and Peg Ryan moving towards him the two uniformed policemen seemed to hesitate, but Larry Smithers of the FBI was already moving towards Peg. Peg seemed to sense his movement, as she turned quickly and took in the scene.

"He assaulted me, arrest him," she cried out, attempting to slide past Larry and the other men blocking the way to the elevator.

"Ms. Ryan, you are under arrest for the murder of Hastings Moment," one of the uniformed policemen stated, while the other pushed her backwards, and away from the closing elevator door.

When the one policeman reached for her free hand, Peg had darted past him, and turned and ran straight for the floor to ceiling window that delivered the stunning view of the Pentagon that appeared to be just several blocks away. She ran straight at the window, as if she had fully expected to be able to shatter the window and jump from the building.

To what?

Ken was sure it was to her death.

But the window did not shatter and instead the woman had hit it at full speed and the window appeared to bow out but then snap back into place, the sound of the collision something akin to a loud pop followed by an equally recognizable sound of breaking bones. However, just as the woman had hit the window, a shadow had exited the woman, and seemingly flown through the window and out into the air beyond the window. It had turned looking at where it had just come from, and Ken saw the shadow seemingly smile, a wide toothy smile and then disappear.

The woman staggered backwards before collapsing to the floor at the feet of the men who had been too stunned to give chase.

Ken stood slowly, feeling the bruised check, and knowing that he was going to have a reminder of the visit for some time. He couldn't help but stare in wonderment at what he had just seen and what had occurred.

"Well, you arrived just in the nick of time," Ken said to Agent Smithers.

Larry was stooped over Peg, examining her. Her face was a smashed mess. Her nose was obviously broken, and several teeth had been broken off in her mouth. Her eyes were closed, but even from here, Ken could see that the damage she had just done to herself was far worse than the black eye, and possibly cracked cheek bone he had suffered from her attack. It was also obvious that she had injured herself even further, as the force of the impact with the window must have also cracked ribs and potentially other bones. A trickle of blood flowed out of her mouth and down her cheek, adding testimony to the destruction Ken had just witnessed.

Agent Smithers' partner stood also to the side, watching.

"Doug, you better call for an ambulance, looks like she's going to have to go to the hospital first," he said.

Ken saw one of the uniformed policemen, toggle the microphone that was clipped to his shirt pocket, and he made the call for the ambulance. Ken made it over to where Larry continued to work on the collapsed woman, trying to make sure that she would survive what they all thought was a suicide move.

"Your father told me you would likely be here. I called him looking for you. We not only found what you expected to find in her house, but we also found evidence of what she has been doing and was planning to do to the Rosewoods. Where's Kristin? Larry said, taking in the open door to the residence.

"She escaped, taking the other elevator down, just seconds before you arrived. I think Peg was planning to kill Kristin," Ken said, pointing to the knife that now lay about ten feet away.

Larry nodded.

"That's what we found in her script. She had written out her plan, but finding you here, I don't think was in it. Your presence probably saved Kristin," Larry said.

"I don't think Kristin has escaped yet, I think there is someone else seeking her destruction that was driving Peg as well," Ken said, wondering whether Larry had seen the shadow that had erupted as if expelled by the woman's collision with the window.

Larry's look told Ken, he had not seen the shadow, or its toothy grin.

"I've got to go find Kristin. Can you take care of Peg, and let me go see if I can catch up with her?" Ken asked.

"Go ahead Ken. We will handle getting Peg to the hospital. You'll need to get your face looked at soon as well. Looks like you took quite a blow," Larry responded.

Ken nodded, stepped to the elevator and pushed the down button. It seemed to take the elevator forever to make the return journey to the top floor.

CHAPTER 17 – HIDING

Kristin heard Peg's voice calling after her, the plaintive sound in stark contrast to the original threatening and fearful voice. Kristin did not stop. Instead she heeded a different voice that told her to run. She was sure that this voice was her own internal voice of preservation, as she now knew for sure that the voice she had listened to for years, wanted her death.

The elevator ride to the ground floor seemed to take forever. All the time during the ride, she expected to be confronted by that voice that had been her companion for years. Thankfully, all she heard right now were her own thoughts. It was only a little before four o'clock, Earl was not scheduled to arrive until five, to allow her the diversion she needed to escape to the meeting with Tony.

She was sure there would be reporters lurking on the 1st floor, so she had pushed the button that would take her to the ground floor where the few cars of the owners in the building were parked. The garage was well lit, and gratefully deserted. She ran towards the stairwell that led up to the outside of the building and onto the street level that ran in front of the building. She exited onto the street and for a moment stopped considering which direction to continue in. She saw the three reporters, with their camera's strapped around their necks, less than a block away. One of them glanced her direction but returned to the conversation with the other two reporters. For whatever reason, he had not seemed to recognize her, even at this close distance. The TV4 truck was parked right behind them, giving answer to how Peg Ryan had gotten to the residence.

Kristin walked in the other direction, turning quickly at the first intersecting street, and looking behind her. She expected that one or more of the reporters would be following her, but no one was. When she had walked another block, something made her turn around again. There was no one there, but she glanced backwards and up at the building, seeing one of the tall windows that marked the foyer of her penthouse unit. At that same moment she saw what appeared to be a shadow seemingly expelled from the window. She instinctively ducked down, beside the car where she was standing. Again, the same voice she had heard that had told her to run, returned.

"Get in the car," the voice said. It was a command, one that she could choose to obey or not. It was completely unlike the other voice, as it had not made any promises like the other voice had, and it had made no demands, simply had issued the command. She took hold of the handle to the back door and the door opened. Kristin did not question the providence that had provided for this car to be unlocked. She slid into the seat and lay on the back seat, trying to make herself as invisible as possible.

Kristin found that she was shaking, even as she began to process everything that had occurred in the last few minutes. She knew that the shadow she had seen emerging from that window, was somehow the manifestation of the voice that now sought her destruction. She reasoned that it would be looking for her, so she slid even further down, sliding onto the floor in front of the back seat. She wanted, no needed to be invisible. Her mind was racing, as she tried to make sense of it all. That memory she had opened in the two hours before the sheriff had arrived returned. She had finally relived her actions with Craig Housher and those thoughts were before her again. She knew there was something there that she had missed or overlooked. She walked through the events with her nearly photographic ability kicking into gear. She relived the various conversations she had with Craig, now nearly twenty-five year ago.

She was at the conversation with Craig, just before her fateful decision to play out the circumstances that would lead to her seduction of him, that she finally focused on.

Craig was explaining his faith to her, explaining his belief that he lived surrounded by spiritual forces, some that were sent to protect him, and others that desired to hurt him. He explained that he was far from perfect, and that sin made him vulnerable to attack. He was explaining why he believed in God, and what Jesus meant to him.

Back then, it had all sounded like nonsense to her. After all she had come to the university not to listen to philosophy or religion but instead to talk about math, science, and what it all pointed to. But most of all, she had come to get Craig away from his wife, his family and to make him want her, the way she wanted him.

Craig had been trying to show her that what he believed all pointed to something greater than what you would normally see and experience. She had pretended to understand, to take it in, but it was all a show for her. She had a goal, and if listening to all of this got her closer to her goal, she would listen.

But now, well, there had to be an explanation for what she had seen and heard, and nothing made more sense than what Craig had been trying to explain to her.

She felt a presence outside the car, and heard the front door open, and she felt and heard someone slide into the front seat, and the door slammed. Terrible fear flowed through her. Was she about to be discovered or was this stranger in for the surprise of their life.

Then she heard his voice,

"Lord, I don't know where she has gone, please point me to where she is running," the voice said.

Kristin could not believe what she was hearing, and who was speaking.

How was it possible, that she had stumbled into his car? Then she heard Craig's voice again, in that same conversation more than twenty-five years ago as he tried to explain to her the difference between karma, that she had told him she believed in, and providence.

"Lord, I know what she has done, yet you have told me through my dad and through Glenn that I needed to make this trip, to speak with her. I know that I didn't want to, that I always thought she was getting what she deserved, but I also know that you have not given me what I really deserve. Give me the words to say to her, and the direction to find her. She needs help Lord, and I believe that is why you sent me here. Not to condemn her, like I wanted to do, but to help her see the truth. Please

Lord, help me, help her."

Kristin felt the car move. He was going somewhere. She wondered whether he was being directed by someone as to where to go, or whether he was just driving hoping to spot her. She just hoped it was away from here. She did not want the shadow to find her, even with him present.

Her mind replayed the words she had just heard. At first, she wondered if it was a trick, and then whether she could use what she just heard to her advantage. But for the first time ever, that she could remember, she rebuked herself for that thought. His prayer had been genuine. Like Tony, he for some reason seemed to want to help her, and he had even less reason to do so than Tony. Tony didn't know her, but this man knew way more about her. Yet, he had prayed for her.

She was too afraid to say anything but the more she thought about the words the more amazing they seemed. A new emotion swept through her, and before she could do anything, she realized she was weeping. She must have made a noise, because she heard the man start, and felt him turning the car rapidly, slowing as he did.

"Please don't stop," she said. "It's me, I'm hiding in the back seat, I don't want the shadow to find me," Kristin said.

To her surprise, the car picked up speed and continued moving away from her home. After a few moments of silence, and few turns with the car speeding up as if to put distance between themselves and her residence, the man's voice returned.

"I think it would be safe for you to sit up, Kristin. They're not like God, they do not know every moment where you are and what you are doing." Kristin slowly pushed herself up from the floor boards and sat on the seat. It took her a minute more to compose herself, until she finally looked into the rear-view mirror and saw Sheriff Ken Farr's eyes, looking at her.

"How did you know this was my car?" Ken asked.

"I didn't," Kristin said stammering.

"The voice that told me to run, told me to get in this car, and I saw the shadow pop through the window of my home, and the door was unlocked, so I got in," Kristin said, as she wiped at her eyes, trying to remove the evidence of the tears that had so suddenly leaked from them. She saw his eyes, again, and she saw the blackening eye, and the swollen cheek. The sheriff didn't seem to realize he had been hurt.

"What happened to you," she asked, unable to contain her curiosity.

"Your shadow clobbered me!" the sheriff said.

Kristin saw him shake his head, and then he said.

"Actually, it was Peg Ryan who hit me, but I think she was getting her direction and strength from the voice."

"Where is Peg?" Kristin asked.

For the next few minutes, Ken explained to Kristin everything that had happened after she had made her dash for the elevator. When he told her about Peg running full sped at the window, with the obvious intent of breaking through it, and the resulting collision and damage, Kristin gasped.

"Was she was trying to kill herself? She'd never have survived the fall," Kristin said.

"I think she was trying to escape, and I doubt that she even thought about what would have been the result if she had succeeded in breaking through the window. And I don't think the voice that was directing her really cared one way or the other. In the end, all they ever want is for us to destroy ourselves," he said.

Kristin saw the sheriff considering her again in the rear-view mirror.

'Sheriff, I'm supposed to meet someone at six o'clock. After I meet with him, I'll go wherever you want me to go. Would you come with me, to meet my friend? I think, you and he have a lot in common, and I will feel better having both of you with me," she said.

Kristin thought for sure he would deny her request, after all, she certainly had not proved herself very trustworthy in the past, even though she had meant every word of what she had said. She had already thought it through and had come to a similar conclusion well before the sheriff had even arrived. She was going to tell Tony everything, and after hearing the sheriff's prayer, well she was going to tell him as well.

She had reasoned that it was better to have a friend who knew everything and could give her honest advice than to try and tough it out on her own.

The voice had known about that thought, it must have, because its near final words to her spoken through Peg, had said as much. It was obvious the voice didn't want her to talk with the sheriff or with Tony and was especially fearful about what they were going to tell her. Perhaps both Tony and Ken knew of an escape that she had not found.

'Where are you meeting your friend," the sheriff asked.

For the first time since Tony's call yesterday, Kristin felt hope. Perhaps she might make it out of this mess yet.

She looked again into the mirror, saw his questioning look, and she told him. A few more minutes passed in silence. It was obvious that the sheriff was thinking about something, needing to say something. But Kristin had questions of her own she needed answered.

"Why did you leave your car unlocked, Sheriff? Did you know that I was going to find your car and hide in it?" she asked.

Kristin saw the smile, and she could feel the sheriff's pain as that smile moved muscles in his face that must be complaining about the activity. She saw him grimace, but saw that it was a losing battle, the smile was winning despite the pain.

"I suspect the same voice that told you to run, and told you to get in the car, told me not to lock the car. Not that I had any clue why I was supposed to do that. I half expected to find the car stolen or stripped bare, by the time I got back. I never expected to find you hiding in it," he said. The smile slowly dissolved back into a serious look.

"Kristin, I'll wait until we are with your friend, but I need you to know, that I am going to tell your friend exactly what I believe you did to Craig Housher. You have a lot of accounting to do, and there are consequences to our actions, even if, we are later sorry for those actions," the sheriff said. Kristin nodded, and then began to speak. She relived the events with Craig, and she relayed everything with the unemotional playback of what her mind had recorded so distinctly. She shared the trip to MIT, the meetings there, her plan and her successful seducing of her former science teacher. His remorse and sorrow, and her disdain of those emotions. She relayed her discovery of the pregnancy, and her belief that bearing his child would change everything for him, but instead it had driven him even further into remorse. She even shared her planning to cover the pregnancy with Buddy House, and her guiding Buddy into a real way to make a lot of money really fast. The unintended consequence that decision had, as Buddy had run faster with the idea that she had imagined he would. Buddy setting up both Craig and another teacher as examples for the other men about to be blackmailed, and the trajectory those decisions put on her own planning. It wasn't too she got to the part of knocking Craig out, using that heavy frying pan his wife had hung in kitchen, and her positioning of Craig on the floor against the couch, that she finally had choked up. She couldn't bring herself to relive or speak the act itself.

"You know the rest sheriff, I killed him. I killed the only man I have ever really loved, and for all these years I have lived off the benefits that came from that act. Later, when my husband had run out of options that I could accept, I thought I had killed him as well. But that you already knew."

'Sheriff, I have to ask, before we meet my friend. Why were you praying for me? You knew or suspected all of this, I don't understand, why would you pray to find me, when you know what I have done, and what I would have gone on doing, if things had turned out differently?", she asked.

Once again, she saw the sheriff's eyes, and they were glistening, the tears obviously just below the surface.

Kristin realized that they had arrived on 9th avenue, and Bobby's was the first building on the corner. True to his word, a very tall, and very bald Tony McIntyre stood beside a ten-year-old Chevy. Dressed in civilian clothes he still stood out like a sore thumb. He had to be one of the most recognizable persons in all of D.C. But everyone flowing on the sidewalk seemed to be ignoring him. The sheriff pulled to a stop, taking one of the few spots that were open for parking.

Kristin looked back at the sheriff, waiting for his answer.

"That's your friend?" the sheriff said, looking at Tony through the window.

"Yes, that is my friend," Kristin said.

The sheriff looked at her again, but this time turning around so he could see her.

Kristin took in the full damage to his face. She knew for certain that he must be in real pain.

"Kristin, I think you probably know the answer already. You see, Craig and I, well we share something in common and from what I know about your friend," the sheriff hesitated to turn and looking back at Tony through the car window before continuing, " he also shares the same thing."

CHAPTER 18 – RUNNING

"I'd like to speak with Tony first, and then if he is okay with it, we will come back, and we can go where ever you think would be best for us to talk." Kristin said.

Ken thought about the request. He doubted that two weeks ago, Kristin would have even given the request a second thought. He had seen her in action. But her words while a statement, belied the fact that she was asking permission. Something had changed within her. He nodded and watched as Kristin straightened her dress further, and then exited the car. He watched through the window as Kristin walked over to Tony and spoke with him. It wasn't long before Tony was locking up his car, and following Kristin back to Ken's vehicle. Tony opened the back door of Ken's car, allowing Kristin to slide back into the seat, and then he had moved to the other side of the car, and slid in beside her. He had to fold himself into the seat but closed the door beside him and looked over the seat at Ken.

"Tony McIntyre" he said.

"Kristin said that she wanted me to go with both of you somewhere, although I wasn't clear where we are going?" He said, as he grasped Ken's offered hand.

"Ken Farr, General," Ken said, as he shook the general's hand.

"Let's dispense with titles for the day, you call me Tony and I'll call you Ken, if that is okay," he said.

Ken nodded in agreement.

Tony looked at Ken's face.

"Son, I'd say you tangled with something in the recent past, that delivered one heck of a wallop to you face? What'd did you do to yourself?" Tony asked.

Ken looked at Kristin and then back at Tony.

"It's a long story, but let's just say, it's one of the reasons Kristin wanted more than just me with her," Ken said.

Kristin smiled sheepishly, and for the first time Ken saw a blush running up Kristin's neck. She hadn't said it, but it was obvious that she had been taken back by the damage that Peg had done to him. It hadn't taken a rocket scientist for him to figure out she wasn't all that confident in the amount of protection he could really afford her.

"Kristin says you're from Hitchenburgh, Michigan, Kristin's home town, is that correct Ken?," Tony asked.

"Yes, that's correct," Ken said.

"By any chance ever run into a Glenn Hitch there, he's from the same town," Tony asked.

The look on Ken's face probably communicated everything.

"Yes, I know Glenn, how do you know him," Ken asked.

"Long story, but Glenn and I go way back, to the Vietnam days. Lots of people know I became a general during that time, but most people don't know the history of that occurrence. A friend of mine was my commander, and when he lost his stars I inherited the job. That's a piece of history no one remembers or talks about.

There was a lot of politics back then, almost as much as now. Let's just say that Glenn was the cause for me becoming a general, and if it wasn't for him, my friend would have been killed, and I would have probably quit the army in disgust. I crossed General Abrams and got relegated back to D.C. for the conclusion of the war, while my friend retired and returned home to his family. I met Glenn one time later, when he visited D.C. to thank me. I haven't seen him in over fifteen years, and other than Kristin, I don't know anyone from Hitchenburgh. How is Glenn?," Tony asked.

"He's fine," Ken said, glancing at Kristin, who was strangely silent, but listening to the exchange.

"What did he thank you for Tony," Ken asked, his curiosity peaked by that comment.

Tony laughed.

'Well, right at the end of the war, I was charged with the review of all military requests for returning to Vietnam. Glenn had posted for a position at the embassy but had been turned down on medical grounds by my subordinates. I just happened to be in the right place at the right time, saw the paperwork, and approved his return. He was supposed to be discharged, after all he had two purple hearts and a silver star already, and according to his paperwork, he had never truly healed from his wounds. But I knew that providence had put me where I was, so that I would see his file and his request. The one thing I was sure of back then, is that if he was asking to go back, someone was sending him, and I was just there to make sure that he made it to where he was supposed to be.

Of course, I thought I had made an error when less than a month later, at the end, I learned that he was MIA and presumed dead. You can say I was more than surprised, when he showed up at my office some fifteen years later, quite alive. I had to thank him. He popped back into my life the same day I had finally decided to retire from the military. It was his visit, that kept me in the service again, and the rest as they say, is history," Tony said.

Ken just nodded, looking at Kristin.

"Where do you want to go?" Ken asked, looking between Tony and Kristin.

"You mean, you don't have a plan already?" Tony asked.

"Afraid not, today has already turned out completely differently from what I'd had planned, so I am open to suggestions," Ken said.

"I know a place about forty minutes from here, where we can go," Tony said.

"It's a park, but it's where I go when I need some solitude, and there's a little restaurant right outside the park that's quiet, but the food is pretty good," he added.

"Tony, why don't we take your car. We can leave this car here, and you can drive?", Ken suggested.

Ken saw that Tony was bent like a pretzel, the back seat of the Toyota just wasn't designed for someone of Tony's size, and Ken thought it would be better having someone who knew where they were going, driving.

Tony's smile said it all.

Together they made the transfer back to Tony's car, with Ken riding in the back seat, and Tony and Kristin together in the front. Once they were moving Tony said,

"Did you know that according to our records, Glenn is still missing in action. Officially he is listed as Killed in Action, his name is even on the Wall, right at the very end as one of the last causalities of the war. Normally, you name didn't get put on the wall unless they were 100% sure you were a causality. Never figured out who screwed up on that. I've checked, and there is no driver's license in his name, no social security records, nothing. It's like he's a ghost, yet I've known for the last fifteen years he's alive."

"He's still alive, even has a family, and that's a story all unto itself," Ken added.

"He has some interesting friends," Tony said.

"Yes, that is one way to put it," Ken added, assuming that Tony was talking about the two angels.

"I am curious, who sent him back to Vietnam, Tony, and what friends are you both referring to?" Kristin said, finally jumping into the conversation while turning to look at Ken.

Ken looked at Tony's eyes in the rear-view mirror, which were riveted on Ken's. In that brief glance Ken saw the same understanding in Tony's eyes that he knew was reflected in his own. Both men had heard in Kristin's tone, something more. They both knew that Kristin understood a lot more than she was letting on.

Ken looked at Kristin, her penetrating gaze not reveling what was going on in her mind.

'Before we answer that question, Kristin, I need to ask you one first," Ken said, holding her gaze.

Before Kristin could answer, Ken felt the sudden acceleration of the car, and Tony cried out:

"Hold on".

The car suddenly lurched forward at the same time Ken felt thrown even harder into the seat as he heard distinct crunching sound as the car was rear ended. Ken looked back through the rear window and he could see the grill of the van behind them, which appeared to once again be racing towards Tony's bumper again. But Tony was still accelerating, and the van came close but then seemed to fall away. Ken saw the strange satellite dish protruding from the top of the van and realized that it was the TV4 van he had seen parked outside of Kristin's residence. Someone had followed them, and Ken had a sickening sense of who that was.

"It's Peg," Kristin said, her voice both shaking and higher pitched than just a few seconds earlier.

Tony swerved and Ken saw the RT 395 sign and arrow wiz by his window. They were moving even faster now, but Ken saw that the van was still in pursuit, although it appeared to be dropping further back.

'Hold on", Tony said again, and suddenly the car was braking and turning onto a ramp, and again Ken saw a sign wiz by, with two words, 'The Pentagon", and an arrow pointing the direction. The van continued to follow. Ken heard the sirens then and realized that following the van there were cars following with their lights flashing and their sirens blaring.

"Kristin, I have a phone in my pants pocket, take it out," Tony's voice steady but with authority.

Ken saw Kristin struggling to get the phone, while Tony continued to steer the car through the curve with the van lurching ever closer.

Kristin suddenly was holding the phone.

"Open it, and press 1991 then the star button," Tony said, once again speeding up.

Ken watched as Kristin performed the task. The phone never rang, but a voice was instantly there.

"General, this is station, what is the emergency," a voice responded crackling over the speaker in the phone.

"I'm approaching the southern entrance, I'm in my Chevy, we have a van chasing us, I need you to block the entrance, do not let us in, I will turn to the waiting area, I need a team there immediately, do what you have to, but stop whoever is in the van," Tony's voice raised an octave higher than normal as well.

Ken looked through the front window and saw they were rapidly approaching what appeared to be the entrance to a parking lot, but even as he watched, he could see barriers appearing out of the ground, as if emerging from hiding, blocking both the access to the parking lot, and to the check points just beyond. Tony was still accelerating.

For the third time, Tony spoke the same words.

"Hold on,"

Ken felt the car begin a slide as Tony yanked hard on the wheel, turning the car while still accelerating. Amazingly the car did turn, and Ken watched as the van closed the distance trying to turn with the car, its bumper just clipping the rear bumper of Tony's car, which sent the car in to an even wilder turn, but the van zipped by the car.

Ken heard the tremendous explosion as the van ran full speed into the barriers that Tony's car had just barely missed, and he saw the van flip and somersault over the barrier, as the sheer momentum and the angle of impact with the barriers did not stop the van completely. Tony's car braked to a stop throwing Ken against the front seat, even as he saw Kristin bracing herself against the glove box and dash board she was thrown against.

"Everyone okay," Tony's question coming at the same time he was already unbuckling his seat belt and opening his door. Ken let out a weak,

'Yes, I'm okay," that was followed quickly by an affirmative from Kristin.

Ken and Kristin followed Tony out of their doors, and Ken held onto Kristin while Tony half ran to where four other cars were coming to a halt, with at least a dozen armed men already closing in on the van.

The van, which lay on its side, it's back wheels still spinning as if the accelerator was still jammed to the floor, but with only air for traction now, seemed to be a living thing, with groans and scrapings still being emitted. Whatever had been jammed against the accelerator must have been removed, because Ken heard the distinct change in the engine noise, followed by the sudden silence as the engine stopped.

The driver's side door, which now faced the sky, flew open and exploded loose of its hinges as if it had been thrown away, as easily as flipping a Frisbee into the sky, and Ken saw a huge black shadow emerge from the opening. From Ken's vantage he could not tell whether anyone else was seeing what he was seeing, but he felt Kristin stagger, and heard her sudden intake of a breath, so he knew she was seeing the apparition as well.

The shadow seemed to look around and then focused in on Ken, and Ken knew, on Kristin. Ken saw the hand emerge from the van, followed slowly by a form, and he saw the shadow seemingly being absorbed back into the form. The woman slowly emerged from the wrecked van, slipping down off the top, where she collapsed to the ground. She was instantly surrounded by the armed men.

Ken moved no closer, and put his arms around Kristin who was trembling, but silent.

Many more men now were emerging from the cars that still had their lights flashing, but mercifully had turned off their sirens.

Ken saw three other men approaching the back of the van, and heard their cries.

"There's someone else in the van," one of the men shouted.

Ken saw the men force open the van door and watched as one man with weapon raised guarded while the two other men opened the door and then reached in to drag out another form.

"We need an ambulance," one of the men shouted.

Already there was a crowd gathering, watching the strange occurrences, and Ken was sure that many of the employees would be talking about this for days. The siren of an approaching ambulance cut through the air, and Ken was surprised at the speed of which it had arrived. It felt like only a couple of minutes.

Ken started to move forward, to get closer, but Kristin shook her head and said, "No, I don't want to go any closer."

Ken choose to stay with Kristin, thinking it better that she not be left alone.

Ken felt the change in Kristin.

"I will not go with you," Kristin said.

"I'm not going anywhere," Ken said, thinking she had been addressing him, but then he realized, that a different conversation was going on, one in which he was hearing only one side. "I don't care about what you can give me and I'm not yours to take," Kristin's voice both defiant, yet even more noticeably afraid.

Ken turned Kristin's face to his own, seeing her eyes already far away, not even seemingly aware of his presence.

"Kristin, don't talk with him, he's a liar, but he's a really good liar. Rebuke him Kristin, don't listen to him. Focus on me, Kristin, don't look at him", Ken said, anxiously waiting for Kristin's gaze to return to him.

"Do not come between me and what is mine," Ken heard the voice, although he saw no form. Ken felt himself thrown as if tossed like a rag doll, but at the same time he felt the slicing pain and gazed down at his chest where a series of slashes suddenly appeared, and great talon's like a birds seemingly emerged from the wounds as he was released and dumped on the ground.

The sensation was between burning and the feeling of flesh being sliced.

At that same moment a rumbling sound echoed around Ken. He heard shouts and turning saw the TV van was ablaze. The men were dragging a body further from the van and towards the waiting ambulance. Without warning the TV van exploded, seemingly lifted off the ground by the force, and a hail of metal and glass shrapnel was launched towards Ken and Kristin.

Ken stood and ran to Kristin. Tackling her Ken covered her body with his own. Ken felt the hard rain of the debris falling all around him, but not a single piece of the fiery remains of the truck struck him, or Kristin. Ken looked up again, and saw the massive shadow standing over them.

"You cannot have her, she is not yours," the words coming with authority filling Ken's ears. To his amazement, he realized that he had spoken the words, and slowly was standing holding Kristin in his protective grasp.

Once again Ken felt the talons surrounding his body, felt as he was lifted and tossed aside again, his hold on Kristin shaken free as if she had been a rag doll in his embrace.

Ken saw the image even better now. It was immense, dark and powerful. It's face seemed to be lit from within with two bright burning yellow eyes, with one eye seeming to be swimming with hundreds of irises. The image stood between him and Kristin, as if daring him to try it again. The image was staring at him, ignoring Kristin, who stood as if comatose. Ken knew he was trying to scare him, and quite frankly he was doing a good job. The thought almost made Ken laugh, and just as suddenly another voice, almost a whisper reminded Ken.

"Resist, and he will flee, for he has no power over you," the voice said.

Ken felt himself stand again and walk towards Kristin.

"The Lord rebuke you," another voice said. Ken turned and looked, and saw that General Tony McIntyre was beside him, his strong arms wrapping Ken and supporting him as he walked towards the shadow and towards Kristin.

No talon's this time, only a strange hollow voice,

"You will not win, you cannot win, she is mine" even as the shadow appeared to be fading.

They reached Kristin, who suddenly awoke from the apparent trance and fell into Tony's free arm.

Ken felt nothing. He did not feel Tony's release of him, or his slow decent back to the ground. His mind shut down and darkness flowed over him.

Ken's next awareness was of light and noise. There were people rushing around him, a mask on his face, and he heard the voices saying, "hold on" almost like Tony had said during the car race, but these words made no sense, and then darkness again.

CHAPTER 19 – CHOICE

Kristin sat in the back of her car. Earl had arrived, after she had summoned him, and she had walked out of the hospital in Bethesda unaccompanied almost fourteen hours after having arrived at the hospital. She had been checked out thoroughly and given a clean bill of health. But her mind was lost in thoughts, and while she had participated with the doctors, answered their questions. It was as if she were two different people in the same body. One person answered their questions, the other person pondered all that she had read, seen and experienced in the last two days.

"Take me home, Earl," she said, and she punched the window button once again sealing herself off from her driver.

She had seen Ken, his badly damaged body bloodied and lacerated. Tony shared what he had seen, even as Ken was being whisked away to the same hospital they were taking her. She heard the emergency personal talking about shrapnel wounds, even though she remembered the seemingly protective shield that prevented any of hot debris from hitting Ken. Ken's body had been her shield.

Tony had directed the ambulances to go to Bethesda Military Hospital, a sprawling complex that had inherited the standard from the old Walter Reed Medical center. It was here that foreign dignitaries, and even the President went for medical needs. Its staff was the best of the best.

They had arrived at the hospital almost simultaneously with the ambulance carrying Ken. It had been a sobering ride for Kristin, as she, Tony and two medical personnel rode in an ambulance carrying the shroud covered remains of her husband. Jim Rosewood had been pulled from the back if the TV4 van, already quite dead. It was clear from his wounds, that he had been tortured before his life had been ended. He had been dead for more than a day already.

Kristin had thought backwards through time. The realization that Jim had died such a gruesome death at the hands of the deranged Peg, cause her to revisit the last few days. She had replayed that final video in her mind and details she had overlooked suddenly came into sharp focus. Her husband's praise of Peg's abilities, her command that he say it again, that she was his number one, way better than Kristin, all came back into view. He had not said those words willingly, he had been coerced. Kristin's thoughts about Jim changed dramatically.

She relived another scene, the final one where she had direct contact with Jim. His,

"You Are!" exclamation when she had asked what his problem was. The weight of those final two words, the last she would hear of his voice in this life, struck home with such force that tears began streaming down her face unbidden. She had chosen to allow his anger and hurt to go unaddressed, preferring her own time of solitude where she could continue to bask in the wonders of that night at the White House. Now she would have given anything to go back and redo that event. But she also knew that there was a whole host of events, of things she had done, that she would now do different. But as her visitor had said, "you cannot undo the past, all you can do is live the future knowing that past actions still have consequences but that you can be forgiven for the past."

Forgiven. What exactly did that mean? She was still learning. It wasn't until the first wave of guilt had swept over her, that forgiveness began to have meaning. Up until that event, she had experienced regret, even remorse, but those experiences had more to do with consequences than the actual events she had done. Now she understood the difference. She had to turn from the activities she had relished in the past. Her visitor had called it repentance.

She thought again about Ken and what she had seen. She remembered seeing the door flying off the tipped over van, and the huge shadow that loomed out of the van followed by the figure of Peg, crawling out of the van, and then falling to the ground. The shadow seemed to be drawn back into the woman, but then she had seen something else, that still shook her. A bright image had emerged from the still form on the ground, an exact duplicate of the woman lying on the ground, except this form's face had no damage. It was as if the dark shadow was pushing outwards this image. The image appeared to be sitting up, with only the face, torso, and arms free from the body.

Kristin remembered watching and seeing the shadow leaving the body and looming over the smaller bright form. The shadow had drawn what appeared to be a curved sword and had swung it. When it hit the bright form, Kristin heard a distinct "thunk" and the sword was embedded in the image. She remembered seeing the image convulse, impaled by the sword. The shadow had lifted upwards and the bright image was yanked completely out of the body, the legs clearly seen. The bright image struggled on the end of the sword, and then the shadow had smiled, as if enjoying the struggling and agony of the image. Kristin heard the sucking sound as the shadows mouth seemed to inhale, and she watched in horror as strips of light seemed to be flayed off the still struggling image. This went on for only a few seconds, but it felt like forever to Kristin. Suddenly the image that had glowed so brightly was devoid of the light. The much smaller shadow of the woman was still embedded on the end of the sword, still struggling.

For a moment, as the last vestiges of light disappeared into the much larger shadow, that shadow actually had taken on a different form. The image morphed into an incredible bright bluish image, with rippling muscles and an altogether more attractive form than the hideous shadow that had preceded it. For those few seconds Kristin felt an emotion radiating from the being, it was satisfaction. But it was short lived, and the light quickly faded from the being returning it to its former condition. A different emotion swept over Kristin, radiating from the being. Kristin recognized this emotion as well, it was pure unmitigated rage.

The shadow had flicked the sword, and the impaled image flew off the end of the sword, but it never hit the ground. Instead the shadow disappeared from sight. As the shadow disappeared, Kristin heard the larger shadow say, "What a disappointment, not even in the top ten." Those words had shocked Kristin. She had heard them before, spoken by Hastings Moment over the phone as he had finished his sadistic torture of one of his victims.

With a certainty that bordered on knowing, Kristin understood now who the victim had been. It had been Peg. With an equal certainty Kristin knew that the shadow had been a participant with Hastings in that torture.

The image turned and looked directly at Kristin. She felt its attraction; this hideous shadow called to her. Images flashed before her mind, memories of all her greatest triumphs. The shadow claimed each of those triumphs as its own and then demanded that she come to him, promising even greater successes in the future.

She remembered saying, "I will not go with you," the words both of fear and a desire for self-preservation.

Then other images, each of the most hideous events Kristin had participated in. The laundry list of destroyed marriages, of blackmailed men and women caught by Kristin in her self- absorbed focus on gaining power and influence. As if that had not been enough, the worst images were held to the end. First her treatment of Chris Rosewood, and Kristin's destruction of that marriage and that family, then the attempt to kill her own husband Buddy, to free her to complete the conquest of Jim Rosewood, and then finally the murder of her teacher, mentor, and lover, Craig Houser. After that final image, the shadow had said, "You belong to me, look what you have done."

Kristin remembered that she had thought, "I do not belong to you," even as she felt as if a ball and chain had been fastened to her very soul. She remembered hearing Ken's words, as if he was calling from a great distance. And then suddenly the shackles had been broken, as Ken had stood between her and the shadow. She had seen the shadows talons fastening around Ken, throwing him aside. The shadow was distracted, giving Kristin even more clarity of the events that were unfolding. She saw Ken standing, his chest a ribbon of slices, blood freely flowing from them, and yet he walked back towards her again. The shadow raged against Ken, its talons again picking the man up and throwing him as if he was a rag doll. But Ken had stood again with even greater damage, and then Tony was beside him, supporting him, and together the two men walked towards Kristin again. It was Tony's voice, "The

Lord rebuke you," that had snapped the final hold of the shadow on her. She heard the rest of the exchange and watched as the shadow disappeared, and Ken collapsed to the ground.

Why had Ken chosen to take on the shadow, to save her? He knew what she had done, and yet he had battled the shadow to save her. She had asked Tony that question, and his answer echoed another voice. "He knew that there was still a chance that you might be saved," Tony said.

That simple statement had silenced Kristin for the entire ride to the hospital. Once at the hospital she and Tony were quickly ushered into the emergency ward, and because of who Tony was, they were seen to immediately. It was only when they got to the hospital that Kristin realized that Tony had been hit by several pieces of the shrapnel thrown off by the exploding van. One piece had actually embedded itself in his shoulder, and for that removal Tony was placed in another cubicle before finally being transferred to a gurney and then pushed into an operating room.

While the medical staff was seeing to Tony, Kristin had sat alone in the cubicle, choosing not to lie on the bed where she had been examined and declared to be okay. She heard everything that was happening around her, and soon zeroed in on the conversation that was taking place just two cubicles away. It was obvious the doctors were working on Ken, and already there were directions about preparing another operating room for him. The doctors all seemed mystified by the wounds they were treating. They were pumping an amazing amount of fluids into him, but kept hearing words like hemorrhaging, and others that made it clear they were not succeeding in closing the wounds and stemming the blood loss. She heard words like, "knife slices," another doctor talking about shrapnel and the damage that should have done. Finally, a much older doctor must have arrived, she heard the deference in the voices of the first two doctors to this third doctor.

"I've seen these types of wounds before, but only one time before. There was a young soldier in Vietnam that was brought in after one of the battles there. He was credited with saving his platoon and the remains of a South Vietnamese division that had been caught in a firefight. We all thought it had to be shrapnel wounds, but just like these, no matter what we tried to do, we could not get them to stop bleeding either," the doctor said.

"Did you lose him?" one of the doctors asked?

"No, we didn't," the doctor responded.

"Well what did you do, how do we help this guy," one of the doctor's voice clearly impatient and anxious about their patient.

"Let's step outside and I will tell you," the older doctor's voice said.

"Outside, you mean leave him alone?" the same voice exclaimed.

"We need to go somewhere, where we are not being overheard, and I will tell you," the older voice said again, with a steely patience.

Kristin heard the three men leave the cubicle.

"You too," the older voice said, and Kristin realized that there must have been nurses there as well. She heard the curtains being drawn around Ken as they left.

No sooner had they left, than Kristin heard the distinct, clack, clack, clack, of someone walking with a cane, or a staff. She heard the curtains open and close again, and then she knew.

She peeked through her curtains and watched as brightness seemed to fill the area, the artificial lightening flickered and went dark, yet the light continued to build emanating from the cubicle and from area surrounding Ken. She saw three distinct images surrounding the bed. Their forms clearly outlined against the curtains. She crept closer sliding carefully by the empty cubicle that had housed Tony until they had pushed him away to the operating room. She peeked through the crack in the curtains, and she saw her visitor and two other forms. The two forms were glowing. One had a deep majestic blue light emanating from itself, the other a paler but equally magnificent turquoise light. Both had turned to her and she realized that they had seen her. She was paralyzed with fear remembering the similarity to the being that had all to recently demanded her allegiance after having stripped Peg's image of light. But these beings said nothing, demanded nothing, instead they turned back to Ken. The intensity of their light suddenly increased, to the point that she had covered her eyes with her hands, and yet the light pierced even those. She had cried out, 'It hurts!", even as she felt herself falling as if a great distance, falling into the light, its intensity increasing dramatically, and she felt the tearing sensation as areas of darkness inside her suddenly were flooded with light. It was as if closets long closed were suddenly torn from their hinges, and great piles of filth were suddenly exposed. She kept falling, and further darkness kept being burned through.

She had woken in a room. She was still fully clothed, laid simply on the top of the covers of the bed. The lights were on, but their brightness seemed dim, compared to the memory of the light she had seen blazing off the two figures. She did not know how much time had passed. She remembered looking around and finally realizing she was not alone in the room. Sitting in a chair just to the side of her bed was her visitor again.

"Today is still the day of salvation for you, but you must choose, and soon, before the day runs out for you. You much choose who you will serve. You will either serve as a princess, or as a minion, as a steward or as a slave. A far greater man than myself said, "Choose this day, who you will serve, but for me and my house, we will serve the Lord. Ken did what he did because he serves his Lord willingly. And Ken's Lord is my Lord. You have been given a great gift Kristin. Few get to see what you have seen, and still retain their sight. Now you must decide what you will do with this gift. You are in a battle, and forces far greater than you are arrayed against you and for you. Choose well, and live," the visitor said.

He then stood, and walked from the room, not waiting for any questions, or giving further explanation.

He hadn't needed to. Kristin's mind was already racing, processing everything she had seen and heard. She had read the book the visitor had given her the day before. It had taken almost eight hours, but her mind with its amazing gift had absorbed those words, and she had spent much of the night and following day considering the words. She remembered a section and relived in her mind the event those words had chronicled. Before her eyes the fiery hosts were displayed, the prophet's simple prayer that his servant eyes might be opened. He had seen a multitude, she had seen only two, and that thought pierced her.

She looked around the room again, wondering about the vision and whether she had been unconscious, if that is what you could call it. She was no longer in the emergency ward but found herself on the third floor in one of the wings of the hospital. No one asked her why she was there, as she made her way back to the emergency ward.

When she walked into the emergency ward, the first person she saw was Tony. He was wearing one arm in a sling, a large white bandage covering a shoulder that was barely hidden under the shirt top he had been wearing. Strangely, he had not questioned her as to where she had been. Instead she had asked the first question.

"Is Ken okay?"

"He's in surgery still," Tony said.

"Surgery?", Kristin asked, confused by the unexpected answer. "Yes, they are still suturing his wounds, but the doctor said he'll be okay," Tony replied.

"But," Kristin started to ask but didn't finish her question.

"You can go in and see him, if you like, "the voice of the older doctor sounded from behind her.

"He just got moved into recovery, but he is quite awake. I wouldn't stay there to long, he needs his rest, he's come through quite an experience, but he will be okay. Based on what I have seen of these types of wounds, he will never be fully healed, but, he will survive," the doctor said.

"Great," Tony said already standing and moving towards the door heading to wherever recovery was.

Kristin, felt his glance at her, asking in that simple facial expression whether she was coming.

"Go ahead, I'll be there in a minute," she said.

Once Tony was gone, she had turned back to the doctor. He was a tall man with a full head of gray hair, and it was obvious his prime days were long since gone. However, his bluish gray eyes sparkled with both intelligence and mirth, and his appraising look at Kristin, told her he knew she had some questions.

'Doctor, I overhead your conversation with the other doctors when you were discussing Sherriff Farr's wounds. Why did you leave his room with the doctors and nurses, and what did you tell them, how did the other man survive his wounds?" Kristin asked.

"He survived the same way Ken will. And I think you know why I took the doctors and nurses away from his cubicle. Not everyone gets to see, what you got to see," the doctor said.

His eyes communicated everything. He knew what had happened, and he knew she had seen it.

"I did not get to see what happened either time, but I saw the consequences and I know that it did happen," the doctor said.

"Would you tell me what you saw, Mrs. Rosewood?" the doctor asked.

For the next few minutes, Kristin tried to explain what she thought she had seen. The doctor had just stood there, listening. His eyes seemed to blaze with greater intensity, but he never had any display of doubt, or unbelief. When she was done he said,

"I've often wondered what the answer to my prayers and of my colleagues had been back in Vietnam. We had so many critically wounded, and so often there seemed to nothing left but prayer, and so often even those seemed to go unanswered. But then, from time to time we would get an especially harrowing experience, and we would be left unsure how to attribute the wounds or the healing that occurred. We all were left with the realization that as good as we were that sometimes the damage was beyond our explanation, and the healing was simply beyond our ability to take credit for."

"My colleagues thought I had lost it all, when I finally stopped and asked them all to join hands and bow their heads. I think one of them nearly had a heart attack when I told him that the way the other man had survived was when several us had prayed for him. Of course, they thought a bit differently, when they returned from my clandestine enterprise. But just so you know, I still believe that it was our prayers that aided in bringing what you got to see. At times prayer is answered with a No, sometimes with a Yes, and sometimes the Lord sees fit to add an exclamation point to either answer. When I saw the Sheriff's wounds, and I remembered what had happened earlier, I thought that once again I was going to get to see the exclamation point, and that is what happened.

"I'll take you to see the Sheriff now", the doctor said.

Ken was swathed in bandages, in fact there seemed to be more bandages than anything else covering Ken's body, and the black eye and swollen cheek seemed to be the least of his damage. When Kristin entered the room, she saw Ken looking at her.

"You're okay?" Ken's raspy question again catching her by surprise.

"Yes, I'm okay," she answered.

Eight hours later, she had called Earl, and now she was headed home. She had relived the day and she had closed her eyes and did something new to her. She prayed. It was a stumbling prayer, but she remembered Craig's voice, and she followed his simple prayer that he had shared with her, but one which she had never prayed before. She prayed for herself and then for the strength to do what she now knew she needed to do, and she found herself praying for her children, for Buddy, and then finally she found herself praying for others she had formerly despised. Tears streamed down her face. Her prayer changed to one of thanksgiving, for the time she had been given. She thought about her activity over the past eight hours. It didn't feel like nearly enough, but she had heard the voice inside her, and she had obeyed.

For whatever reason, she had felt the need to write it down. In eight hours, she had written out over ten letters, all but two were over five pages long, the ones to her children were the longest of all.

Her prayer changed to a question, why had she been given this opportunity while so many others with so much less sin and guilt had not.

She heard the answer, again, Craig's voice filling her ears. 'The one that is forgiven much, loves much".

"But why me, I don't deserve it," her prayer again, shadowing her soul as she poured out her understanding of what was happening.

"Because I love you," she heard his voice clearly again. That same voice that had told her to run, told her to get into the car that turned out to belong to Ken, that had told her to write. That voice, as crystal clear and as compelling as any voice she had ever heard.

She felt the change in the speed in the car and opened her eyes. The voice spoke softly to her. "Fear not, I am with you," it said, and Kristin felt peace flooding her being.

The road zipped by and she realized that they were not headed towards Arlington. Instead they seemed to be on a five-lane highway and the speed of the car was continuing to build. She pressed the button, lowering the window.

"Earl, you're going the wrong way," she said.

The head turned looking at her, at the same time she saw the gun that his hand was holding. Except it wasn't Earl's face, that was staring at her. Kristin recognized the blank manic eyes that were staring back at her, all semblance of reason gone from them. She also saw the car beginning to swerve into the lane, the driver now completely distracted from the task of steering.

"I see that you no longer want what I can give you," the voice said.

Kristin recognized the voice immediately. It was the shadow, but it was coming from the driver of the car. She felt the car as it side swiped the semi-truck, the loud blaring of the trucks horn as that driver responded to the seemingly out of control limousine. Kristin felt the car lurch back into the lane, and the driver momentarily seemed to look forward getting the car under control, but its speed continued to build. Kristin head the blaring of the trucks horn, its squealing brakes as its driver struggled to regain control of the truck

His face turned again, the manic grin still there, as was the gun.

"I told you, I would get you for what you did to me," the voice of the man said, the gravelly voice replaced by the real man's voice.

At the same moment Kristin saw the limo was gaining rapidly on another semi-truck.

"Avery, I am sorry for what I did to you, please forgive me," Kristin said.

Avery's face seemed to contort, and his shout was a mixture of both his own voice and the gravelly voice of the shadow.

"You're sorry! You're sorry!" Avery screamed at her.

At that same moment Kristin heard the gun fire and felt the impact of the first bullet in her chest. He fired again and again.

She looked at Avery feeling as if all the air in her lungs had been expelled by the bullets. She looked into his eyes and mouthed the words, "I forgive you, Avery" even as he started to turn, realizing the approaching danger. Whether he had understood what she had tried to say, she didn't know.

Kristin felt the impact of the limousine with the next truck and felt the car as it went airborne, while the truck body seemed to begin to wrap itself around the car. Avery's scream turned from anger to panic as he suddenly realized that he was no longer in control of the car. Kristin looked down at her chest, seeing the three holes and realizing that she had no ability to breathe, as if a huge fist had slugged her. Everything seemed to slow down, there was incredible amount of noise, crunching, horns, and strangely what sounded like music. Her last thoughts were a prayer, "thank you, thank you for allowing me the right choice.

CHAPTER 20 – DEATH OF A SAINT

K en sat on the end of his bed, the scrapbook resting on his legs. He was dressed and ready, his best dress uniform on. Normally he would have worn a suit, but for some reason today he had felt the need to wear his best uniform, it was as if in his uniform he would be able to honor the man who in his mind held a rank far superior to his.

He was still struggling with what he was going to say. They had asked him, if he wanted to say anything, or just remain silent, lost in his own thoughts and memories. He had chosen to speak, the man he honored would have wanted it that way.

He opened the scrap book his father had given him only a few short weeks ago. The scrap book chronicled his father's life, but Ken knew that his father had started the scrap book after the destruction of the first parlor in Hitchenburgh some twenty years ago. Twenty years. It did not seem possible that so much time had passed.

Ken looked at the first page of the scrap book. Pictures stared back at him. It was a picture of his father as a child, being held by Ken's grandparents. Ken had never had the chance to meet them, but he knew them through the stories his father had shared with him. His grandmother looked severe in the picture, but Ken realized that it was from a time when smiling for a photograph was actually frowned upon.

Ken's father had shared the stories about his grandmother, and that she was light hearted and jovial as was his grandfather. Both were the children of immigrants. His grandfather family was from Holland, his grandmother family from France. His grandfather had been raised Dutch Reformed, his grandmother came from the French Huguenots, although she had been raised as a Methodist. His father had been one of four children, but only he had lived past the age of twenty. Two of his brothers had died in the Second World War, his only Aunt had died of polio as a child.

Ken flipped the page, and a picture of his father and his mother Abigail on their wedding day, followed by a picture of his father in flowing robes as he accepted his degree. This was followed by a picture of a church building with the congregation standing outside, his father's first church. Then another picture, of another church, one that Ken recognized, the small house to the side the place he had called home for all his youth. Another picture of his parents holding a small child. Ken recognized himself. Both his mother and father where much older in that picture, and he remembered the stories both parents had told him. He was a child of their middle age, past the time they had expected to have children. He turned the page, and a death notice of his mother, with her picture, and then the notice of the approval by the board for the construction of the Parlor by a vote of three to one, with one abstention. On a page all by itself was a rose petal, under it his father had written. "So that I never again forget."

Ken knew the story of the rose petal. It was perfectly preserved, as if it had been embalmed like the pharaohs of old, but unlike them, it had no wrinkles or graying. It still looked like it had been picked yesterday, and its' loneness did not diminish the fragrance to this day that it gave off. His mother had loved roses, and the scent reminded him again of his walks through her garden and the multitude of roses and the sheer wonder of the sensation.

He flipped towards the middle of the scrap book, and a newspaper clipping regaled the details of the destruction of the Parlor in Hitchenburgh, the headline blaring, "Freak Lightening Kills Hundreds at Parlor". It had been forty, but it just as well could have been hundreds, the sorrow of his town had never been deeper. Nine of the forty had been from Hitchenburgh; some were friends that he had known well.

Another photo showed him in his police uniform with a picture of Beatrice just to the side of that picture, with announcement of his engagement, another picture showing their wedding, performed by his father, and then a picture of him in a suit after his election as police chief and then finally one of Beatrice holding their first daughter Abigail Faith Farr, named after his mother, everyone called her Faith as Abigail seemed to be an old fashion name. Only he and her mother called her Abbey. She had turned sixteen just last week. They had celebrated that event with his father as well.

Again, Ken flipped forward several pages, and stopped riveted by the headline.

"VP Candidate Jim Rosewood Found Murdered."

Another clipping, apparently from the same newspaper, said "Kristin Rosewood dies in car accident."

Ken read that account, remembering the emotions that had flowed over him, now over ten years ago. Had it all been for nothing? That question had been his first reaction to the news of her death.

In the weeks after the events, the news media had a seemingly unfailing cornucopia of news items about everything that had occurred. The search of Peg's house had turned up all the evidence needed to confirm her involvement in Hasting Moments' death. She had kept the hundreds of names removed from the trophies discovered in the plane after Hastings death. Those names displayed both Hasting and Avery's involvement in so much crime and wickedness.

That list resulted in resignations, more divorces, and other civil actions as almost three hundred lives were turned upside down, as the names became public. There were even three suicides, and each person was hounded unmercifully as the press looked for more confirmation of exactly what had been done, and what had been promised in exchange.

The news media barely covered the other discovery made at Peg's house. It turned out that Jim Rosewood had not filed for divorce from Kristin. The papers that had been delivered to Kristin were fake. There was no law firm by the name on the envelope, and in fact, Jim Rosewood's signature was probably the last act he had done, before Peg had killed him as well. Her obsession with Kristin was amazing, and only because Kristin, not she, held that unenviable first spot in the brothers strange demented measurement of their own enjoyment of their victims.

Her "breaking news" of the divorce was made up. There was some speculation as to how long she would have been able to keep up the ruse. But Ken was sure, it would have gone on a lot longer, except for the unexpected changes within Kristin.

The death of Avery Moment, in the same accident that killed Kristin, left the press mystified. The details of the three bullets found nestled in the body armor that Kristin had worn under her dress, were never released to the press.

Ken had wondered out loud to his father whether there was any reason for the body armor that Buddy had given her, if she instead would die in the accident, just shortly after being shot by Avery. Certainly dead, was dead, regardless of how it occurred.

Ken's father had only smiled, and said one word, "Time".

In the end, what had happened between the time Kristin was shot, and the time she died in the wreck, would have to remain a mystery. In Ken's mind, all the suffering so many had experienced, appeared to be for nothing. That hurt more than he would admit. It was one thing to suffer with a known outcome, another to suffer not knowing what had happened in the end.

The press did latch onto the details of Peg's escape from the FBI, and Avery's escape from the hospital where he had been transferred for observation. The stories on their escapes seemed to elevate both of those individuals to the notoriety of a Bonnie and Clyde, although neither had ever been seen together, and their exploits had been independent of one another. Those stories kept the news media busy for weeks.

The details of Kristin's own financial dealings and her involvement with Hastings and Avery never made it into the newspapers after her death. It was as if the relationship no longer mattered. The bureaucracy had no desire to have the hot potato of Kristin's activity the center of any ongoing media speculation. The "what to do with the over billion-dollar estate left by Avery" was decided quietly. Surprisingly, it was left to Avery's daughter Susan, and as a complete surprise to everyone, she had not wanted a single cent of it. Instead she had directed that a trust be set up and all fines and costs for the ongoing legal battle with Kevin Hill be paid from it. Whatever would be left, would be sent anonymously to more than three dozen mission groups she and her brother had picked for support.

The remains of the TV 4 van also had been a treasure trove in what it did not reveal. Inside were found melted together several large memory devices, all from Kristin's apartment. When that fact was released, with the statement that nothing was salvageable, a collective sigh of relief was heard all over Washington.

That led to a three-month period, where all sorts of people started claiming to have been involved with Kristin, as if, being a notch in Kristin's black book was suddenly something to be desired. Most of the accounts ended up being proven false, but several high-level resignations, both in the court system, and in other federal agencies, were reported as continuing fallout from the scandal.

When Ken woke in that hospital room staring up at the bright countenance of Benjamin, alongside Glenn and the other angel, it was Benjamin who had spoken,

"Well done, Steward," his words again filling Ken will peace, as if he had finally discovered his purpose.

It had been the second time Benjamin had called him Steward. Once again that title seemed to elevate his own understanding of just how much importance he had. The other angel that Ken always regarded as the quiet one, once again said nothing, but drew from her side a bright sword and handed it to Benjamin, who in turn laid it beside Ken on the bed.

The sword shimmered and then faded into a staff that now lay out of place on the bed. Ken moved his closest arm, and his hand grasped it. As he grasped the staff it changed again, and Ken studied its new form and understood. He had seen it many times, and he had held it often, but never with the appreciation that he now had. Its' worn leather binding, and faded gold leaf edges, were familiar, and he knew, it was his fathers'. He looked at it and asked,

"Does my father know?"

He looked at Glenn who rested his head on his two hands atop the staff he held. The staff morphed as well, and soon Ken saw that Glenn held a similar book. Tears filled Glenn's eyes.

"I never knew my father, but he left me his book as well. For years I ignored it, and left it in a drawer, while I wore his memory around my wrist," Glenn lifted his arm displaying the watch that still was fastened around it. "Finally, when I was injured and sent home to heal, I found his book in that drawer, and his notes in the book.

Craig Housher, became my guide, explaining parts of the book that I struggled greatly with. Craig was a young man then, only a few years older than me, and newly married, Julie was expecting their first child. It was in his living room that I learned the truth. He is my father in faith, for he was present as I was birthed into the Lord's kingdom. My father's faith became my own. Often this has been a staff to bear my weight when my frailty seems more than I can bear, and other times it is a sword both to defend and to wage war for the truth. But it is always a reminder of my father's faith in, and love of the Lord who gave these words as a gift and a guide to those that He loves."

"Your father knew the battle you were entering. He sent it, to help in that battle. It will serve you well. You have begun a long journey my brother. Ahead of you stand experiences that will fill you with so much wonder, that at times you will want to just go away and pray and mediate on all that you have seen and been a part of, and other times with so much sorrow, that you will plead that He will take the responsibility away from you, but you will persevere. Your wife and your family will suffer with you, but they will also be your home, your retreat. They will not be immune from the experiences you will share, but they will be protected."

Glenn's words came as if from a deep well of experience, a mixture of joy and great sorrow seemingly swimming all around him. Ken felt it all. Ken understood, that something had changed in him. He no longer had to wonder what Glenn was feeling. He knew what Glenn felt. Glenn's smile at the end though had flooded Ken with a sense of awe. He understood now what his father had spoken, everything in this life existed in two planes simultaneously. It was the physical world, seen and felt, and it was the spiritual world, felt, heard but mostly believed in. He had been given a glimpse of the spiritual side, the veil had been lifted for the briefest of moments, and both the glory and the struggle he had seen would be with him the rest of his life.

Ken looked at the next page in the scrap book, at the folded piece of paper. It was a short note, and he had never seen it before. He opened it and read.

Beatrice found him still sitting on the bed, his eyes closed, with tears leaking out of them. He felt her arms slide around him.

"Are you okay?" she asked.

"Not really, I miss him so much, and he has only been gone three days," Ken said.

Now was a time for truth, not platitudes. He knew that Beatrice would understand, probably better than anyone would.

"I miss him too," she said, he arms circling his head and holding him to her bosom.

"Not all tears are bad," she said. He often said that to me, as he liked to quote from one of his favorite writers.

Ken nodded, and felt comfort surrounding him in her embrace. He finally sat back up taking in his wife's face. She had matured even further, and if it was possible, she was more beautiful today than on the day they had been married. The two tears that rested on her cheeks bore witness to the truthfulness of the words she had said to him.

"We need to go," Ken said.

Beatrice nodded.

"The kids are ready, and Julie Housher is waiting with them downstairs. I told her she could ride with us.

Ken nodded and stood, picking up the two sheets he had found in his father's scrap book and picked up his father's bible, that he had been given that day in the hospital. He had been given answers to his questions. He knew what he was going to say, and he now knew that the battle had been worth it. He held the proof of both within those two folded sheets and in his father's bible.

The service was traditional in format. John Housher had led the congregation through several readings. His father had asked that the service take place back at Grace Presbyterian. The small church would only seat three hundred, and there were more than a thousand in attendance. The elders had set up hundreds of chairs outside, with even more packed around the church. Even so, many would be standing outside, listening to the service and the words that were being spoken over the make shift loud speakers hoisted up on their metal poles.

The casket had been open for several hours before the service, and many had filed by giving final tribute to the man that now lay so silent and still. As with so many funerals, Ken knew that often people looking down on him, would remember a living man, and suppose that the man in the casket was not him. But it was him.

Finally, it was Ken's time, and he stood to walk to the pulpit, where John greeted him with a bear hug and whispered words, "He is with the Lord!"

Ken nodded and then finally stood in the pulpit where his father had preached for thirty-five years, and he looked down at where his father now lay. He looked back up at the congregation, his wife and children in the front row, followed by many friends and families. Glenn and his wife Mylinh and two of their children and all their grandchildren were there, as were many others. The elders from the First Presbyterian Church, where he had served until only a year ago, when they had finally called a replacement pastor, were here. The entire Day family, with Scott and Teresa now married, with three children now. It was the Day's oldest son Patrick who now served as pastor of First Presbyterian. It was as if that crucible of fire his family had passed through had prepared him for his role leading that church after Ken's father.

"I am the son of a pastor," Ken began.

"My father taught me much about life, and about faith. He was a man of prayer. I know that some of you know, and for as long as I remember, Tuesday's were a day of prayer and fasting for him. As I look around this church, I can honestly say that of those I know, not even one of you were not at some time lifted up by him, in prayer and most of us were lifted up many, many times.

I know I certainly tested his patience, as did some of you. Some of you are sitting on pews that are missing a fair number of screws. I know, because I removed them, over a period of eight Sunday sermons, when I was six years old. Despite all his efforts and mine, we never did find what I had done with all of the screws. He often wondered whether I ever heard his sermons, as I always seemed to be somewhere else as he spoke. I know I was a matter of prayer and much fasting for him as well.'

The chuckling that had started erupted into laughter, as Ken delivered that line.

"He was not perfect.

I watched as his faith was tested by the death of my mother Abbey. Nothing shook his faith more, than that event, I think. It was the first time I saw him rocked to his face, knocked off his knees, which is where he normally would be found in prayer. He actually fell asleep here, in this church, in that isle," Ken pointed to the center aisle, "as he wrestled with whether his ministry had meant anything. I think he was close to losing his faith at that point. But, the Lord's promise was that he would not snuff out the smoldering candle or break the bruised reed. My father was a testament to the truth of what the Lord has promised.

Ten years ago, most of you know, I was in my own battle. One of our own, from our town, had done some horrendous things. She had seemed to be rewarded for her scheming and wickedness and was close to becoming our nation's second lady, and I know she had her eyes on the first spot. I was sent by my father to her, to confront her, but also to let her know that she still had time to turn from what she was doing, and who she was in league with. That trip cost me a lot. I ended up in the hospital for almost six months. I wondered whether it had been worth it, whether my father's prayers and direction were misguided.

I wondered what I could say to you all today, that would bring any meaning, any purpose to us gathering to remember by father. I know some of you, meaning well, have said to me, "He isn't really there," Ken pointed to the coffin.

"And in some ways, you are right, a part of him, isn't there, but instead he rests with the Lord, and with my mom, before the Lord. But you are also very wrong. That is him lying there, it really is him, and as he would tell you, that," again Ken pointed to the coffin, "is the confirmation of the truthfulness of God's word. Death is the curse of sin. My father was fond of saying that everything in this life reflects a spiritual reality as well. The creation itself points to the creator. Every struggle in life, every illness, every success, everything has a spiritual dimension as well. You see, you and I we are body and soul. We see the body, we live in the body, we are the body, but we are much more. We were never meant to be divided, but sin brought a sting with it, that sting is the division of what should not be divided. That sting is death, the divorce of body from soul. My father is here, and not here.

Was my father's faith, false?

Would it have been better for him to enjoy more of what this life might have offered him? He was a smart man, he could have made a lot of money. Instead he chose to live on what a farming community could offer to a pastor. He never went on any fancy vacations; he never had anything but the cheapest of cars. If I ever heard him complain, it was that he had never been able to afford to give my mother anything more. I still remember my mother shushing him, when he had those doubts. She would tell him, she had everything she had ever wanted, and when he would look confused, she would kiss him, and say "You, you dummy!"

I found this letter to my father, in his scrap book, this morning. I had never seen it before. I had heard that there were other letters sent to folks. I know that one letter lifted the despair of a woman in our midst, who discovered that her husband really did love her, and their son more than anything, other than the Lord, and that he had not committed suicide."

Ken had asked Jenny of he could mention that event, when they were alone while Beatrice and the children were walking to the car. He had not explained why he needed to mention that, but she had nodded her permission.

"I felt that something good had come out of the suffering after all, and that my father's faith was true, when I heard about that letter. At least my confrontation had led to clarity to that event that had been so sorrowful for her family. But, inside, I still wondered if that was enough to make it all worthwhile. But then I found this letter to my father, and now I know that it was, and that my father's faith, and your own, is worthwhile,"

Ken picked up the two sheets and began to read,

"Pastor Farr, You and I have only met a couple of times. Your son told me that you sent him to me. I know he came as the sheriff, looking to solve several crimes, but I also know he was sent to warn me about the end of what I was doing.

The two times I did meet you, both times you told me that there were many who were praying for me. I suspect, but cannot know for certain, that the many probably could be counted on one hand, maybe two if I am particularly generous. Certainly, few had much reason to pray for me.

I can't explain everything that has happened, but I wanted you to know that your prayers, and the prayers of the others had a result. If you are reading this, it means I never got to tell you in person or share with my family what has changed. It means that my past did catch up with me, but now I no longer fear the past, although I did, do, fear owning it.

It also means that the Lord knew of my fear of having to own everything I have done in this life and decided to spare me and so many that display. Like the thief on the cross my coming to belief will have been witnessed by few. There are so many I am sure he would have wanted me to tell, and there are many that I need to tell.

The last two days have been a marvelous discovery for me. When I was young I wrote a paper that was an open door that I could have walked through. Craig Housher tried to walk me through that door. Instead I chose to close that door, instead choosing what I thought I wanted even more. At the end of the work, I asked a question. I asked, with all of the proof that I am able to present, the mathematical certainty of what I have just proved, I cannot answer the question of "why" what I demonstrated actually is true.

In the last two days I asked the same question, "Why?" Why would anyone willingly take on the penalty for what I have done? And I found the answer. He told me, and I heard his voice, "Because I love you." I have not slept in two days, thinking about that answer that I found in the book you gave Glenn, to give to me. I am in the hospital, and I experienced that answer again, as I looked at your son, lying on his bed, because of me. I finally felt love and what it means. I do not understand it, but I love this Lord, who would send you, and Ken, Glenn and my son, and even Buddy into my life. Your book finally explained that to me. All of this, knowing completely what I have done. Even when I finally admitted my need of Him, and my love for Him, I asked Why? And his answer was right there, in front of me. "Because I loved you first."

"I left your book for your son. You see, I have been given a gift that I have ill used in the past. The words are now embedded in my mind, and the more I dwell in them, the more the darkness flees from them and from me. I now know what it is the darkness fears. It fears His words. It fears the light. It fears love. And so did I for so long, but no longer. Thank you. Kristin.

Ken looked up at the congregation, and then down at his father.

My father sent his bible to Kristin. I did not realize that until today. I received it after that act had fulfilled its purpose. My father is a pastor, our Lord is the Pastor. The Pastor's promise is that all who call on the name of the Lord will be saved. Kristin learned that truth, and I know that as truth. That is all my father ever wanted for any of us, that we might know the truth, because the truth sets us free. That is why we are gathered here to remember him, and that is what I will always remember most about him. All he ever wanted is for us to know the one who had saved him and set him free.

He stands now with the Lord, and my mother, and a host of others who have gone before us. We are gathered here so he might hear before the throne of our Lord, our voices saying, "you were and are a good and faithful servant and many are those who believe because you were faithful." I am sure though, that there is one voice more than any other that he is listening to, and that is the Lord's.

The Lord's promise is that my father's body and his soul will be reunited. That is the greatest promise of all, that sin's sting will be removed, and death will not reign. That he will be resurrected, body and soul reunited forever, the way it should be, that is what I am looking forward to. Today we remember my father. Then, I will stand with my father, body and soul in one place, together in perfection and know perfectly the truth, and the full meaning of the words, "I love you."

Ken looked down on his father again, and then stepped from the pulpit. He stepped to the open coffin, slipping something small under one of his fathers' folded hands. He had taken it as well from the scrapbook. Even hidden under the cold and stiff hand of his father, Ken could smell the scent of roses.

EPILOGUE

Ken stood gazing up at the tree.

Susan House had directed a gift from one of her trusts to remove the dead tree, and Henry Drake had been more than happy to finally remove that tree, even grinding away the roots. Not a speck of that tree was left after Henry was done. Ken had bought the replacement tree himself. With Henry's help they had planted the sapling sugar maple together.

The sugar maple tree was already well over twenty feet tall. Last year, for the first time, he and Beatrice had gathered tree sap from it. Its two pails full just enough to make about a quart of maple syrup. When Ken had heard that the land was available the year after they had replaced the tree, he had asked Beatrice for permission to buy the tract that included this tree. Like so many farmers, the owner of this land was making the parcel available for development. Ken had not wanted this piece of land to go that way yet. There were just too many memories tied up here.

After they owned the land, he had put three large picnic tables under the tree. It was not a bit unusual for him to see visitors and strangers stopping at the spot and using the picnic tables to eat their lunch or dinner, not realizing that the property was not public property or realizing what had happened here. People tended to be a bit messy, so he had added a sign, encouraging them to clean up after themselves. That had helped, but again, he often found himself at the site in the morning, picking up any trash that had been left behind. It felt right, letting the spot being used, even if it was inconvenient at times.

It was not uncommon for Henry and his wife Sally to join Ken and Beatrice every year here. It was the event of the removing of the first tree that had brought Stephen, Henry's oldest son and Abigail together for the first time. They had known of one another, but they had gone to different churches, and were two years apart in school. For Ken, providence remained a great mystery, but he had accepted that event, and their developing fondness for each other over the years.

Every year, on this same day, he had made it a tradition to come with Beatrice and his children to the tree. Now with three grandchildren of his own, he would regale them with the stories of his father's life, and the events that had unfolded around him. He never spoke of his own experiences, unless he was asked directly to do so. He much preferred not talking about those experiences. Being with family here, sharing his father's story helped him get through this most difficult day each year.

Abigail had married Henry Drake's son Stephen, who like his dad had continued in the tree business as well. They had two children already, and a third well underway. Both he and Beatrice were happy that Abbey and Stephen had made Hitchenburgh their home and not moved away, like so many families experienced these days. It was a new experience being called "granddad", by his grandchildren.

Their son Tom was away at school for his final semester of work. He had finished up his four years of college, going to the same school that Jim and Susan House had graduated from. He was now at a small seminary in Greenville, South Carolina, following in his grandfather's and father- in-law footsteps. He had married his high school sweet heart, Caroline Julie Housher, John and Chi's third daughter. Tom and Caroline's first son, Jerry Farr, named after Tom's grandfather, was already a year old. Tom already had a call waiting him, and unlike Abigail, he would not be staying in Hitchenburgh but would be moving to Baltimore to pastor a church there.

Jim House had pursued the ministry, but not as many had thought. As he had said during his graduation speech he had been ordained, but only after he had also earned his medical degree. Jim was serving as a missionary and doctor in Uganda, Africa. When Buddy House died, Jim had flown home and led that memorial for the man that had become more of a father for him after discovering that he was not his real father.

Buddy had settled back into Hitchenburgh and lived his final days a constant companion of Ken's father. Glenn Hitch visited often as well and was there for Buddy's memorial service.

Susan House had been true to her word. It turned out that the federal courts refused to consider their appeal to the Michigan Courts' decision. Two years before his father's death, Kevin Hill had received a little more than two million dollars as his reward for the law suit he had brought. His celebration was cut short, as he died of a heart attack less than a week after receiving the payout. Ken had heard that there were four women contesting for ownership of the estate. Alison Day was not one of them. Alison had never married, but her daughter was away at college, and Alison lived close to Theresa and Scott Brown, and they were as close as family could be.

Ken's father's only comment about the award and Kevin's death, was a paraphrase from the scriptures,

'What does it profit a man, to have gained everything the world has to offer, only to lose his soul."

Susan House was a practicing attorney but had declined a political role, when she had been offered the opportunity to run for the open senate seat representing her district. Instead she had founded several non-profits and was busily working to try and prevent pornography in all of its forms, from getting any further hold in Michigan communities. She had done all of that, not touching a single cent of the money left to her from her real father's estate. What remained from that estate had gone to the charities as promised.

She simply was a very successful lawyer, and her nearly photographic memory made her a terror to anyone trying to take her on in the court setting. Already she had two cases slowly making their way through the court system. It was interesting watching and listening to her argue the balance between freedom of speech and the dignity of womanhood. She expected to lose, but she was making sure that everyone knew what was at stake. Liberals and conservatives alike ran whenever they saw her coming. Her arguments were too logical, and too sincere, even if they could not agree with her. Her conclusions scared the heck out of her detractors. She simply drew a straight line from their practice to the logical result.

Ken's father's health had been failing, and it had been a blessing when Patrick Day had been called to take over the ministry at First Presbyterian. After all, his father was eighty-four years old. That had to be a record for an interim pastor. Fourteen years.

His father had been fine, a little frailer every day, but his passing had still been a shock for everyone. Ken now knew that his father had been expecting it and had been preparing for it. Less than two weeks before his death, he had passed on the scrap book to his son. The night before his death he had told Ken, he needed to read it, and to pick up where the story left off. It was as if his father had known that he would struggle with what to say, and that Kristin's letter would help him find the words. It was also possible that his father knew that the suffering of the next day was going to be different than all the other times.

Every year, on this day, the lacerations he had received over twenty years ago would mysteriously flame up again, as if they were threatening to erupt and leak again. There was only one year that this mysterious reminder of his battle with the shadow had not occurred.

It was the day that he had found his father dead, in his bed some ten years ago.

They had dinner together the night before and had spent the time talking about everything that had occurred and the suffering Ken expected he would experience again the next morning. His father had laid his hand on his shoulder and prayed for Ken, asking the Lord to provide his son with the strength to get through the next day.

However, the next day had come, and the wounds had not flared up, like they had every year in the past since the event and ever year after his father's death. It was when Ken had come to tell his father that news that he had found him peacefully laying on his bed. It was as if the Lord had known, that was all the suffering Ken could take at one time.

Ken decided to retire from being police chief. He had served in that role for almost thirty years and felt that it was time to do something else.

This would be his last week serving in that role, and he had flatly refused to endorse any of the candidates that were popping up all over to wrestle for the job. Next week this time, he would be the former police chief. Beatrice was happy with that decision as well, but Ken was wondering what he was supposed to do as a fifty-five-year-old. Somehow, becoming a farmer just didn't feel right.

So, here he stood looking at the tree, praying and asking what he was supposed to be doing. The rest of the family would arrive soon. He had wanted some time alone, to pray and think about the past and the future. The tree was truly magnificent, its branches stretching almost as wide as its height. His eyes were still riveted on the tree, when he felt his presence.

Ken turned, and saw Glenn Hitch standing there, resting on his staff. Ken looked around, hoping but not expecting to see Glenn's companions. They were not there, and Glenn shook his head confirming what Ken had suspected.

"Glenn," Ken said, waiting for what he knew must be coming.

Glenn smiled, reading clearly Ken's expectation.

As normal, after a few more seconds, Ken could not wait any longer.

"I have been wondering why I was led to resign my job. Beatrice thinks I want to retire, but I haven't told her what I think I am supposed to be doing," Ken said, again waiting for Glenn to fill in the gap in his thoughts.

Glenn smiled again.

"I don't think you have ever visited Atlanta before, have you?", Glenn asked.

"No, I've never been there," Ken said.

"Well, there is a new business there that an old adversary of ours has interest in. I have been directed to go and check it out. I was told to take you along," Glenn said.

"So now, I am an apprentice," Ken asked.

Glenn smiled, again."Something like that, but a little further along, you already know what we are up against," he said.

'A fifty-five-year-old apprentice, "Ken said shaking his head and turning hearing the arriving cars. He watched as Beatrice, Henry, and a few other cars approached.

Ken nodded as he watched the cars arriving.

"You'll stay to help me explain to Beatrice what I will be up to," Ken asked, turning back to Glenn, but he was nowhere to be seen.

He waited for Beatrice to be alone, he needed to tell her. Finally, while everyone else was playing around the tree, he finally started to tell her, she had laid her hand against his mouth.

"I know," she said.

"How?," he asked.

"Hanna told me," Beatrice responded.

"Hanna?" Ken asked. "Yes, Benjamin's partner filled in the gaps in my understanding" Beatrice said.

"She told you her name?," Ken asked, filled with wonder at the emotions he felt radiating from his wife, and at the knowledge that the other angel had communicated with his wife.

"Why?" Ken added.

Beatrice just smiled up at him, a sad but resolute smile. Emotions of awe, concern, sadness, hope and love flowing out of her. So many seemingly contradictory thoughts, at the same moment, were swirling around in Ken's mind, Beatrice's emotions only adding to his own confusion.

Beatrice wrapped her arms around her husband, her mouth touching his left ear, and Ken heard her whisper:

"Let's just say that I've been praying as well, and the Lord answered my prayers.

Ken relaxed as understanding flooded his mind.

He kissed his wife and remembered his first kiss when he was ten. Beatrice eyes were filled with tears, and Ken felt and knew she was remembering the same event.

Kens' mind added to his wife's explanation, "Yes, he has answered our prayers, with an exclamation point!"

PREQUEL

A Peak At The Next Book By Charles de Andrade Available June 2019.

Eyewitness
"The Tears of the Saints"

How does one describe ones first sight?

I remember seeing my hands, dark shadows suddenly taking on form, with water drops running along the fingers, with light streaming through the gaps in my fingers. Then, I saw the water beneath me, the ripples caused by the falling remnants of water from my hands, and then a figure of a face staring back at me from the pool still disturbed. I saw a man with a black beard, with black hair, tanned skin and green eyes staring back. I saw myself.

How can I explain to you what happened next? Would you believe tears? The tears of a lifetime flooded from my eyes. The tears that had been denied me because of my condition now flooded through the lids I had just gained. Tears of sorrow, of abandonment, of hurt and of anger, and finally of love and wonder surged forward and replaced the water that I had used up only recently. I sat there crying and suddenly realized another emotion so seldom experienced, that of thankfulness.

Would you understand why I looked up into the sky, saw blue for the first time, and the white of clouds? Would you understand why I looked around quickly and saw for the first time two individuals who had come to the pool as well for washing? Then I saw the baked brown and white of the buildings surrounding the pool, and the gray of the stones of both the road and some of the other buildings. I know the people at the pool thought I was crazy. They were right. I splashed in the water, sat in the water, and stared up at the sky and I wept. The tears once denied me were now running without aid. I was whole.

A shudder passed through my body and I knew something else. There was something still missing. Looking again in the water I examined my eyes closely. There was no mud left on my face, and where before there had only been hollowed cavities with missing orbs, there were two greenish pupils with whitish orbs. How can I explain to you what I looked like before? I cannot! I can only guess what I looked like before. But I can tell you, that my face was not pretty to behold. Where my eyes were supposed to be were instead empty sockets. I had been born blind, but this was more than just blindness from lack of ability, it was blindness from lack. The teacher had made two eyes from spit and dirt, and now I beheld what I had not been given at birth. I know that my whole face had changed. Its shape and contours were more normal now, as the hollowed-out depressions were now filled in.

My doubt had been replaced with fact. The teacher not only could restore what was lost, like what he had done for Simon and Jacob, he could replace what had never been given. With that thought, I stood knowing that I needed to return quickly to the teacher. I needed to tell him what had happened and to thank him. I needed the answer to what was still lacking from my life. I needed to know the answer to the question I had not been able to ask. " Who are you Teacher?" raged within my soul.

I needed to tell my friends and my family. My heart was bursting with need. I stood and rushed out of the pool area. But I was lost!

I knew how to get here blind, but now in the light everything was so different. I had trusted the feel of my feet and hands before but now with sight it was as if those senses had ceased to exist. I stood confused as to which way to go. Finally, I forced myself to close my eyes. Fear welled up within me that perhaps I would not be able to open my eyes again, but when I did, the light continued to steam in. I closed my eyes and waited for my sense of direction to return. It finally did, and I opened my eyes and followed where my feet and hands directed.

www.ingramcontent.com/pod-product-compliance
Lightning Source LLC
Chambersburg PA
CBHW031230260626
47169CB00007B/2232